I0553198

HER SWEETEST DOWNFALL

A NEW ADULT PARANORMAL ROMANCE NOVELLA

REBECCA HAMILTON

EVERSCORCH

Her Sweetest Downfall © 2015 Rebecca Hamilton

All rights reserved under the International and Pan-American Copyright Conventions. No part of this book may be reproduced or transmitted in any form or by any means, electronic or mechanical, including photocopying, recording, or by any information storage and retrieval system, without permission in writing from the publisher.

This is a work of fiction. Names, places, characters and incidents are either the product of the author's imagination or are used fictitiously, and any resemblance to any actual persons, living or dead, organizations, events or locales is entirely coincidental.

Warning: the unauthorized reproduction or distribution of this copyrighted work is illegal. Criminal copyright infringement, including infringement without monetary gain, is investigated by the FBI and is punishable by up to 5 years in prison and a fine of $250,000.

ABOUT THE BOOK

Her Sweetest Downfall

She's marked for a life she doesn't want. He's tasked to make her comply.

Ophelia's been successful at hiding her true identity, until the mark of the serpent appears on her neck—a death sentence, should it be seen by anyone in her town. Hiding the mark might save her from falling victim to the witch hunts of her era, but the scorching sensation it carries can't be ignored.

When the mysterious Ethan is sent to collect her for a life of something more, she learns concealing the mark is the least of her worries. She's destined to don a new mask—to join a dark, supernatural world and protect the future of people she may never meet.

What she doesn't know—what she learns too late—is that her initiation won't be complete until she kills the man she loves.

GREAT PAXTON, 1808

OPHELIA KNEW two things for certain: First, the mark where her neck met her shoulder was not there yesterday, and second, if Lady Karina caught sight of it, she would hand her over to the church.

Initially, the marking seemed to be nothing more than a dark outline of a circle. But as Ophelia leaned closer to the mirror, her hand balanced gently against the frame, she realized the mark formed an ouroboros—a serpent eating its own tail.

Her heart sunk to her stomach. The town would make no exception of her; she would suffer the same fate as Alice Russel, declared a witch and murdered in a fury of violent outcry. No matter that no one could possibly know what such a marking meant—that it came from nowhere was enough to declare it evil.

The brass doorknob rattled, and she startled.

"Ophelia!" came the edge of Lady Karina's voice. "Open this door."

"One moment, please, Miss."

She quickly started buttoning the front of her copper gown, but Lady Karina continued rattling the door.

"I'm coming in," she said.

The tinker of keys echoed through the thin wooden door, and Ophelia's fingers stumbled with the buttons on her collar, her heart racing faster with each passing moment.

The key slid into the lock, then the knob turned. She finished the final buttons of her gown and spun toward the door, pulling the two muslin flaps of her apron over her shoulders and starting to pin them together behind her neck.

Lady Karina stepped into the room, an envelope clutched in her hand. "You are *never* to lock your door," she said, her irritation visible in the tremble of her long blonde curls. Her gaze trailed down to Ophelia's neck. "Your collar is a mess and your buttons are one off. We can't have that, can we?"

Ophelia tried to steady her hands enough to smooth the collar of her apron. "No, Miss."

Lady Karina let out a crisp sigh and impatiently tapped the envelope against her arm. "Well? Are you going to straighten up? Surely you don't expect me to do it for you."

If she undid the buttons to fix her collar, she would expose the serpent—the devil's symbol. Women in this town had been killed for less, and each execution delighted Lady Karina more than the last.

Stepping back, Ophelia covered the buttons with her hand, lowering her gaze to the floor and away from Lady Karina. Ophelia never much liked to make eye contact with Lady Karina anyway. The first time they'd met, Lady Karina had told Ophelia that her large, ice-blue eyes gave her the willies.

"I'll take care of it right away, Miss."

"Very well," said Lady Karina. She handed over a small envelope with large script on the front. "Deliver this to Lord Isaac. He'll need it by tomorrow morning, so you must make haste."

Ophelia offered a polite nod, taking the envelope and

tucking it away in the deep folds of her apron. "I'll set out immediately."

"After you make yourself a bit more presentable, of course," Lady Karina corrected. "Percy is preparing one of the horses."

Lady Karina stepped out without so much as a glance back. Once alone in the room, Ophelia spun back toward the mirror with a sigh.

"What 'ave ye gotten into?" she muttered to her reflection. "Father would go mad."

But Father wasn't there. He'd never know his daughter had turned herself over to the same life as her mother, the same life that Father had worked so hard to put behind them. He had hoped for a proper education for her, as the poor lagged behind the upper class in education. Ophelia was reminded of this every time she spoke, and her accent had become so ingrained over the years that she soon tired of trying to speak properly. Her wisdom would show in other ways, she hoped.

Father had wanted more. He hadn't known the way things would change following his death, the way their estate would dwindle, his daughter forced to start anew. A proper education was out of the question now.

Ophelia, however, had not taken this work for the pay. No, she'd done so because she was certain Lady Karina's brother knew something of the disappearance of her mother, who had worked for him two years prior. Gone to work for him, and then disappeared. Ophelia found her way here just six months later.

This job—it was all a lie, a masquerade designed to find her mother. Wherever she had gone, Ophelia knew she would not have gone willingly—not without telling her daughter why she was leaving. Ophelia would not stop this hunt until they were reunited, until her mother could once again hold her in an embrace and make the world feel right again.

After checking the marking once more—it had darkened and the skin had raised slightly—Ophelia did her buttons up properly, pinned the flaps of her apron collar up in a more acceptable fashion, and covered her hair—black as sin, as Lady Karina said when they'd first met—beneath a cream bonnet. She wrapped her mother's old knit shawl around her shoulders and set out into the chill of autumn.

Atticus waited, saddled and bridled, stomping his foot against the cold earth and shaking his mane as he sneezed the early evening air.

"Many thanks, Percy," Ophelia said to the young man holding the horse's reins. "I'll take it from 'ere."

As she rode into the woods, the horse's canter thudded the ground like the beating of tribal drums, and the sap-scented wind shushed between the leaves above. In the distance, between the oaks and maples, a violin played.

She dug her heels into her horse's sides and set him into a gallop. "Come on, old boy. We don't want to be 'ere when night falls."

Already the autumnal sun was low, its sharp light slicing through the breaks of the forest canopy and glinting off the crystallized stones embedded along the forest path. Night would fall too soon.

Damn her. Lady Karina would never travel these woods at night, nor would anyone sane send their maid unattended for such a task. Not with the highwaymen known to pass through, not knowing the things those men would do to a woman alone in the woods.

When darkness encroached, there were still a good few miles left to Lord Isaac's estate on the other side of Blackwood Forest. Thunder rumbled, but the heavy air did not yet spit down rain. She'd need to make haste. At least word had it that Lord Isaac often permitted late night visitors to stay the night in his servants' quarters.

4

Atticus slowed to a trot. Up ahead, white feathers scattered the forest path.

"Come on," Ophelia said. "*Come on.*"

Wolves howled from somewhere deeper in the forest, and the horse stopped.

"Atticus," she hissed. She dug her heels in. "Go, boy."

The horse whinnied and took three steps back, shaking his head. She stroked his neck and lifted her gaze to scan the forest. The moon glinted through the lattice of leaves only enough to reveal the dark trunks of the thicket on either side of the path. Above, charcoal clouds streaked against the patches of night sky, moving shadows over her forest path each time they rolled past the moon.

With the night came a chill nearly as cold as a winter morning, her breath puffing from her lips in a cloud of smoke. The violin tune grew louder; it cried mournfully between the oaks and maples like the wind in the tree boughs. Her chest tightened. How could that be? She'd covered too much ground to still hear this same violin.

Atticus reared, tumbling Ophelia from his back to the forest ground. He stomped his foot and backed away.

"For goodness sake!" She stood and dusted leaves and debris from her dress. When she reached for his reins, the horse stepped back further.

"*Atticus,*" she hissed, and she lunged for him this time, snatching the reins. But just as soon as she'd recouped her horse, he bolted away, ripping the reins from Ophelia's hand with a burning force. Atticus thundered back the way they'd come, leaving her alone in the dark.

Tears and cold night air stung her eyes. The violinist must have been terribly near because she could hear the tune cutting through the trees and underbrush. She glanced back over her shoulder for Atticus, but he was long gone.

As she shuffled toward the edge of the path, the overgrown grass soughed together between her shins. "Hello?"

The mark between her neck and shoulder ached, and she placed her hand on it, the pressure a near relief.

I need to get to Lord Isaac's estate.

As she treaded across the decaying leaves along the trail in search of her horse, a clammy chill rushed up her spine. She stole one last glance into the woods. Yellow eyes glowed between the brambles, and her breath rushed from her and left her lightheaded. Her throat felt dry, and she tasted something rotten on the wind.

Quickly, she spun back around, desperately searching for her horse. Before she could so much as orient herself, something hooked around her waist and knocked the air from her lungs. A rough hand clamped over her mouth, imparting the tangy spice of cloves on her lips.

She choked on the saliva in the back of her throat and threw her elbow into the person behind her—a man, judging by his strength and the mass of his arms. He grunted, but didn't let go.

FROM GREAT PAXTON TO DAMASCUS, 1808

As THE MAN dragged Ophelia into the underbrush, she struggled against his grasp. His hand fell from her mouth, and she sucked in a breath, prepared to scream. But before any sound could pass her lips, he hoisted her over his shoulder and broke into a sprint, weaving through the forest so impossibly fast that the bark and leaves became a blur. Their bodies thrust into darkness, black and complete. A sudden surge left Ophelia with the feeling of her stomach lagging behind. A light, bright and blinding, flashed before them, and they slammed to a halt.

He lowered Ophelia onto something, and she blinked a few times to clear her vision. She was on a bed, and they were in a cabin with strange walls made of mortar or packed clay. Before she could get out any words, her stomach churned. She rolled to her side and vomited on the floor, then fell back against the pillow and closed her eyes.

The man said nothing, just allowed her to rest. He shuffled and rattled beside her, likely clearing away the mess. But the bile still coated Ophelia's tongue and teeth, and her stomach's previous contents permeated the air with foulness.

"Why——" Her voice cracked.

Her question was rewarded only with silence. Even with her eyes closed, the room spun.

As soon as she regained a sense of balance, she would look for an escape. She needed to remain calm—to find out who he was and where he'd taken her. Even highwaymen could be persuaded with enough charm, though she had her doubts about him. Most would rush to rob a woman of her belongings or innocence, but he had not yet done so.

"Who are you?" she asked, her voice gravelly. "Where 'ave you taken me?"

The man's footsteps creaked across the floorboards, and his hand, warm as sheets stacked beside a fire, brushed her hair away from her neck. He unpinned her apron and started on the buttons.

This was all wrong. If he were going to take her innocence, he wouldn't bother with the gentle care of unbuttoning. She pushed her hand against his forearm, but her effort did nothing to stop him. As she attempted to sit up, dizziness rushed to her head, and she fell back again.

He pulled the top of her gown past her shoulder, and his fingers grazed the burning mark between her neck and shoulders.

"I was right," he said, his voice deep, husky. It was the voice of a man who lived away from a society of formalities. He stood and paced away.

A new panic thumped through her. The serpent. If that was the reason he'd brought her here—

Ophelia blinked, and the small, bare room slowly came into focus. The cramped structure made her stomach go cold. She lay on a cot beside a window that was clearly too small to climb through. The only door was on the opposite side of the room, which seemed to be all the cabin consisted of, aside from a kitchen along the wall across from a humble fireplace.

Between Ophelia and her exit, the man crouched at the hearth, his body angled toward her, his sleeves pushed up to his elbows. The flames cast a warm glow over his tanned face and forearms, and his dark, overgrown hair tangled in front of his deep brown eyes.

"I do not intend to harm you," he said, stoking the fire.

He pulled on his collar, straining it against the other side of his neck. Right there, just at the apex of his shoulder and his neck, was the same mark of the serpent. "The ouroboros is said to represent rebirth. To protect against evil. But it doesn't."

He turned toward her. "We are mediators between the physical and spiritual world. *We* are the ones meant to protect against evil."

"I think ye 'ave the wrong idea, sir," Ophelia said, managing to sit upright. But, deep down, she knew the identical markings were no coincidence. "Now if ye don't mind . . . "

She stood and headed for the door, her heart racketing in her chest. The man didn't move.

"Going somewhere?" he asked.

She wobbled near the doorway, gripping the doorframe for balance. "I've a letter to deliver."

"That, my dear," he said, "is going to take you a very, very long time."

Outside the door, the land stretched out toward nothing. Just acres of dried grass, the world a wash of pale yellow in the moonlight.

She spun back toward the man. "Who are ye? Where 'ave ye taken me?"

The smile fell from his lips, tension settling along his shaded jaw and the corners of his eyes. "Please," he said. "Sit."

"I'm fine standing." The burning on Ophelia's neck grew more intense, and she pressed her hand there to ease the sting.

"I can help," he said, "but you have to trust me."

"Do I?" she asked, narrowing her eyes.

"If you want that burning to go away, yes."

She continued out the door, thankful the air had warmed. She must have lost her shawl in the struggle.

Which way to go?

"You'll never make it back on foot from here," he called through the open door.

"Well, certainly not if I stand 'ere talking to ye!"

She started off, heading toward a horizon that glowed red like a fresh cut. She would go as far as she could before the night swallowed the sun. Maybe civilization was not too far past the horizon. She would find out where she was and how to get home—if Lady Karina's estate could even be called such a thing.

Not to mention there'd be hell to pay once Lady Karina found the letter had been lost. Perhaps Ophelia might like this new town, stay there a while.

But something wasn't right. Where were all the trees? The houses and people? The plant life was sparse and silver in the moonlight—not the usual greenery common to England. Even the air felt different here—warmer, heavier—and the breeze lacked the scents of oak and pine.

Ophelia righted the buttons on her gown, but left her apron unpinned. Her leather, high-button boots crunched across the dry grass, and a second pair of feet shushed behind her. She crossed her arms, about to turn around, but the man grabbed her first. Before she could take another breath, they were back in the cabin. It felt as though she'd fallen and thudded to the ground, but she was still standing.

"Ophelia," the man said softly.

A lightness rushed to her head, and her heart fluttered, be it from nerves or the sudden change of location or just the gentle timber of his voice. She tilted her head, but couldn't turn enough to see him. "Ye know my name?"

He reached past her and closed the door before releasing

her. "I was sent for you, and, frankly, you're better off with me. You won't make it back to Great Paxton from here."

"Won't I?" she asked, turning toward him. She narrowed her gaze, scrutinizing how this man could have gotten her back into the cabin so quickly.

"No." He stepped too close for comfort. "You won't. You're thousands of miles away, in Damascus, and you've travelled through time and space to get here. Going back is impossible."

Damascus? Did he think her so foolish as to believe such a claim? She straightened her shoulders, refusing to back away, refusing to let him see the nerves that tingled in her chest and stomach.

"Nothing," Ophelia said, "is impossible."

The man smiled, amusement crinkling the lines around his earthy-brown eyes. "Good to hear that, as it will make my job much easier. Please, just sit with me for one hour and listen to what I have to say. After that, I will leave you alone, if you wish."

Ophelia huffed.

"One 'our," she said sharply. "And only as I need ye to explain where I am and 'ow to make my way back to the forest."

DAMASCUS, 1808

WITH THE DESCENT of night came a chill. Ophelia huddled by the fire, a tattered wool blanket pulled tight around her arms. The man, who had introduced himself as 'Ethan Forrester of Rome' sat a foot away, his elbows resting on his tucked-up knees.

"Ye do not truly go by Ethan, do ye?"

The man chuckled. "Of course I do. You are referring to my origins, I presume. I was born Etán, but became Ethan over time. Forrester was my family's name; they were British. I, however, hail from an orphanage in Rome."

He said it lightly, like being abandoned by one's own family meant nothing. Ophelia didn't know how to respond.

"Do you know what became of your mother after your father's passing?" he asked.

"My mother? What do ye know of my mother?" Ophelia's inner walls shot back up. How could he possibly know anything about her family?

Ethan set his deep, maple-brown eyes on her. "They've been watching you since your arrival at Lady Karina's estate."

"Who's been watching me?" The burning on Ophelia's

neck was so intense now that even the pressure of her hand would not ease the pain.

"Forgive me," Ethan said. He reached for a small bowl of red fluid near the fire and scooted closer to her. A small cloth rested in the wooden bowl, one corner stained by the contents. "Let me ease the sting first. Then I will explain."

As he kneeled in front of her, the fire casting his shadow over her small frame, her heartbeat quickened. Given his sudden proximity, his shoulders seemed wider, his physique more rugged. Ophelia repressed her urge to touch his arm and instead clasped her hands tightly in her lap.

Ethan rested the dish on the ground at her side, and she swallowed, lifting her eyes slowly to meet his gaze. He stared back for a long moment, then cleared his throat.

"Do you mind?" he asked, touching the top button of her gown. "I'll need to treat the welt directly."

The gesture was entirely inappropriate, yet with the pain working deeper into her neck, Ophelia found she didn't want to move—didn't want to risk the rub of her gown against the burning mark of the serpent.

The idea of him seeing her exposed in any way stirred unease in her stomach, but when she looked up at him, at his warm, gentle eyes, her worries came undone. She froze, unsure what to do, somehow persuaded by the pain of the serpent's mark and the man's close, gentle proximity.

Finally, she nodded, dropping the wool blanket from her shoulders to the floor, and held her breath as he slowly unbuttoned her gown. His fingers lingered on each button, his hands trembling. His demeanor suggested a gentleness—a concern—but his shallow breaths suggested something more, perhaps an effort to control a more intimate desire.

Ophelia's heart raced, and when he reached the button between her breasts, her breath caught in her throat and warmth spread across her chest and up to her ears.

It was not fear she felt then, not as she should, but rather an attraction to this strange man from whom she knew she needed to escape.

"I don't wish to make you uncomfortable." Ethan averted his eye as he finished unbuttoning her gown halfway down to her navel. He grabbed the wool blanket and draped it around Ophelia's midsection, allowing her to ease the gown from her shoulders and slip out of her chemise and stays without exposing her breasts. "Perhaps a drink would help?"

Ophelia smiled weakly. "Please."

Ethan poured her a glass of wine, which she drank quickly and set aside. She couldn't seem to escape his stare, the way he looked at her as though he wanted to take her in all at once, to absorb everything from the hair framing her face to her very soul.

She stared down at her lap, trying to focus on the moth-eaten holes along the edges of the woolen blanket.

"Your mother"—Ethan dipped the end of the rag in the red fluid of the bowl—"she was taken the same as I've taken you, but not for the same reason or by the same people."

"She's alive?"

He pressed the rag against the mark, and Ophelia winced, but soon the fluid cooled the sting. "I'm sorry. She died not long after."

Tears bit at Ophelia's eyes, and her short-lived hope wilted in her chest. For a moment, she thought this man might be able to help her find her mother. Instead he was lying to her, trying to get her to give up, to throw her off track. Her mother *couldn't* be dead.

"I won't hear any more of this," she spat, slanting her eyes toward him. "None! You are a liar, and a sick, vile man to lie of such a thing!"

Ethan stared back but said nothing, and Ophelia's chest ached with an unnatural weight. Would her mother be gone this long without sending word? Ophelia shook her head. She couldn't entertain these thoughts. Her mother could very well be prisoner somewhere, stuck wherever she was as Ophelia was stuck now. But dead? If Ophelia believed that, there would be nothing worth living for.

Ophelia rose to her feet and glared at him. "Ye are a horrible, vile man."

Ethan stood, and Ophelia stepped back. He approached, touching her shoulder as she pressed her hand to the serpent's mark.

"Ophelia," he said gently. "I know this grieves you—"

With her free hand, Ophelia pounded his chest once, pushing him away. "Ye don't know anything about me! Or my family!"

He advanced again, this time pulling her to his body before she could hit him. She dissolved into tears, crying hard against his chest as he held her there. He smoothed a hand over her hair.

"I'm sorry, Ophelia."

Lord, she knew he was speaking the truth. She knew in her heart, as much as she wished to deny it, and she'd known for a long time. Ophelia was no fool. Women who went missing for long periods of time, such as her mother, never returned. And perhaps the same fate would befall Ophelia if she didn't push her emotions aside and focus on her own predicament.

"And why 'ave ye taken me?" she whispered, trembling now, stepping back again.

"This world is filled with evils that stretch beyond the darkness of humanity. You and I"—he rubbed the stubble on his jaw and breathed deeply—"we've been selected for a reason. And we are not alone, all of us marked with the serpent."

Ophelia pinched the bridge of her nose and closed her eyes. This man was unstable. "I need to leave, now, Ethan. I appreciate the help with . . . " *the serpent's mark.* She raised her gaze to meet his. "Let me see your mark again."

Ethan pulled at the collar of his shirt, revealing the mark on his own neck.

She studied it more carefully this time. Yes, indeed it was identical to her own. She bit her lip. No, this couldn't be right. She shook her head, gaze steady on Ethan, a sudden boldness swelling in her core. "Ye did this to me! Tell me 'ow ye broke into Lady Karina's estate—into *my* chambers!"

"Ophelia, you're in no danger. Don't you think I would have hurt you by now if I planned to? I could easily restrain you and stop you from leaving—and I will, if I must. But for now, I request you sit and listen."

She didn't sit.

Ethan sighed and sat by the fire himself.

"When I was called, I heard a drum beating. I was lying out in the pasture, and the sound was so demanding I could *feel* it." He glanced back to Ophelia. "I followed it, and that is how I met my guardian. I found her where the music led, though she was not the one playing. No one was. I know you heard your song, too, Ophelia."

The violin. But he could be making that up. Though if he were, he made for an exceptional liar. Ophelia sat on the floor a few feet away from him. "What is it?"

"The music?" Ethan raised an eyebrow. "It's how you know. Your calling."

"And if I *still* don't know?"

"Some people ignore, some evade, some deny. But you always know."

"Maybe ye are wrong."

He sighed, stretching his legs out in front of the fire, crossing them at the ankles. "I will tell you of those that are marked, such as we are. The Universe chose us because of our heritage—because we were born to dual breeds."

He couldn't possibly mean . . . "I've only heard the term once before. '*Dual-breeds*'. My mother—" Her throat tightened, but she swallowed the pain and continued. "My mother spoke of them in the fairytales she told me as a child. 'ow did ye know of 'er stories?"

"They aren't *stories*, Ophelia." He rubbed his temples. His hands were chapped, as though he'd spent months in the cold or working outdoors. "What did she tell you?"

"She told me about the elementals. Cruor were Earth, I remember that. Strigoi were Air—no, that's not right. Water. The Ankou were Air. There were others, too, yes?"

Ethan nodded. "Chibold for Fire. And in more recent centuries, we've had the Witches as well."

"I was enchanted by Mother's stories. Sometimes terrified."

Ethan shook his head. "At least she told you," he said. He wrung the cloth and started again with fresh red liquid on the mark. "I was completely in the dark until my guardian came."

"What 'appened to 'im?"

"*Her*," he said. "She was killed in the war, trying to protect me."

A war? Hadn't her mother mentioned a war? Not in her stories, no—it'd been something Ophelia had overheard her mother talking to her father about. Ophelia had been sitting by her bedroom door, holding her breath to listen as her parents spoke in hushed tones in the kitchen. She came out of the room, asked for a glass of water. Her mother smiled then. Weakly.

Ophelia shook away the memories and returned her gaze to Ethan. "What war?"

"That's why you're here." He pushed the fluid back toward the fire. Here, so close to him, Ophelia could see the fire reflecting off the golden flecks in his eyes. "The dual breeds are under attack. Your mother was one of them, as was my father. They were dual breeds who mated with humans, and for that, you are one of the chosen. As am I, having been born to a man who was part Cruor and part Strigoi and a woman who was human. While having at least one human

17

parent has rendered us both human from birth, we've always had a connection to this. Now we must take on a new form and work silently to help save the dual-breed races."

Ethan spoke of Ophelia's mother's stories as though they were real, and unease swelled in the pit of her stomach. "I'm not sure what ye are attempting to imply. What does any of this 'ave to do with the serpent's mark? Or why ye took me here?"

"Once our kind—those of us who are marked—accept our calling to work for the Universe, we might help restore peace among our races."

Among our races? The pit in her stomach grew to the size of a large squash. "Ethan, please. What *are* ye talking about?"

"Otherwise, we all die." He leveled his gaze at her. "Some of us sooner than others."

DAMASCUS, 1808

Ethan looked over to her with those deep brown eyes, as though seeing her for the first time. How did this man know so much of her mother's fairytales? Why would he try to convey these ideas as any kind of truth?

She pleaded at him with her gaze, silently begging him to stop talking such nonsense. *Elemental races?* Ophelia scoffed and glanced toward the door, contemplating running from him, from all the things he was saying to her.

His expression melted into something softer, and he closed his eyes. "I apologize. I counted too heavily on your knowledge from your mother's stories. Please understand there is no easy way to say this. You will hear this now, but you will not accept it until much later. I just pray you do not fight it for long, because we don't have much time."

"Time for what?"

"Let us start at the beginning, please," Ethan said. "You expressed some knowledge of our world—the elemental world. Put aside your mother's stories for a moment. Do you believe in a higher power?"

Ophelia eyed him slowly, taking in the sincerity of his expression. Even with the scruff along his jaw and the haunting quality of his eyes, she could see he was a gentle man.

"I do," she said finally.

"Do you think this higher power would want good things for the lives of humans?"

"Of course."

"Yes, of course," he repeated. "Shortly after humans were put on Earth, the Universe—this is what I know as our higher power—found that there was an evil on this earth as well. This evil consumed some of the humans, and those humans brought harm to others. This is when the creation of the Cruor came about, because, as you must understand, the Universe can only create. It cannot destroy."

"Cruor, the earth elementals," Ophelia interjected. "They were born from this earth, people once buried alive. They feed off the life of 'umans by drinking their blood. Sunlight can kill them. Legends."

This was her understanding from her mother's stories, but how true it was, Ophelia still had her doubts.

Ethan nodded. "These are not just stories, Ophelia. This is the history of our world. I will show you."

With that, he reached behind him and pulled a knife from a sheath located at his hip. Ophelia's entire body tensed, and she leaned back. She'd misjudged him . . . relaxed her guard too soon. She needed to wait in calm until she knew exactly what he was doing, but she also needed to be ready to sprint for the door in the event it wasn't anything good.

"Take an apple from the dish on the counter and bring it here," he ordered.

Ophelia wasn't going to argue with a man holding a knife. On her way back with the apple, she glanced at the door again. Now might be the perfect time to—

"I won't hurt you, Ophelia. Now bring me the apple and sit down."

Warily, she sat in the same place as before and rolled the

apple across the floor to him. He laughed as it teetered to a stop by his knee, and Ophelia's cheeks burned. She shouldn't be embarrassed to be afraid of this man, but she was.

"Fine," he said lightly, "I'm terrifying. I'm—what did you call me earlier?—a horrible, vile man!"

Ophelia scowled at him. "Ye wanted to show me something?"

"Yes," he said, still with the laughter in his voice. "Look here."

He cut the apple open and showed Ophelia the huge rotting spot on the flesh inside, between core and the skin. "What do you see?"

"I see . . . ." She stopped as he brushed his thumb against the rot and held it there, the apple beginning to . . . heal? . . . before her very eyes. "That can't be."

He quirked his eyebrow. "How can it not be, Ophelia, if it has just been?"

"But . . . " She narrowed her eyes at him. "Then what are ye? This is not what I know of the Cruor."

"I am not one of them," he said. "My father was part Cruor and part Strigoi, yes, but the Universe has called me to be something else. No blood drinking or shape changing. Those who are marked with the serpent must take on the form chosen for them, as we cannot become one of the elemental races of our parents."

"Why not?"

Ethan rubbed his brow, eyes closed, then dropped his hand to his side. "Igniting one of those parts of us would also bring to the surface the rest of what lies dormant. We'd become dual breeds as well."

"Where did ye learn all this?"

"My guardian taught me, as I am teaching you now that you are my ward. When the time is right, every ward is told the mission they are to achieve. Mine was to become a guardian myself, and that is I why I am here for you."

"When did your guardian find you?"

"I was an orphan. My parents had believed it would be my best chance in life, to grow up as a human. I ran away when I saw the mark, and my guardian came to me shortly after that. She found me hiding inside an abandoned cart on the road."

"Ethan, that's horrible. How could they leave ye?"

The corner of his mouth tipped up. "Don't think of that. Either way, I would have been destined to an empty life had my guardian not found me."

"But 'ow do ye trust your guardian has conveyed the right mission to ye?"

"The Chibold receive messages from the Universe. The guardians report to them."

"Chibold? The fire elementals? Aren't they only children?"

Ethan frowned. "It worries me you think of them as children. Most appear that way, yes, but appearances are not everything."

Somewhere deep down, Ophelia had always known these things. Ideas perhaps taken on from her infancy, from before she could form things into memories, into visuals and words. The stories that had always felt too real to be fairytale. How would this man know these stories, lest they were true?

"What about ye, then? Ye could not become Cruor or Strigoi. Clearly ye are not one of the Chibold. And the Witches are all mortal. Only the Ankou remain. Or are there others?"

"There are other sources of magic in this world, but only five elemental races, so yes, I'm one of the Ankou. We're bound by night to move the Morts, the spirits of the dead, to ensure they do not overtake a human's body and cause further destruction."

"My mother said the Morts caused the witch hunts." That was part of the story. Part of that dark fairytale her mother had told her so many nights while sitting by the fire. If what

Ethan said was true, daylight would be the true test. Daylight would reveal his nature, reveal those gossamer wings the Ankou were said to have, visible only in the sun's direct rays.

Ethan nodded. "But it's not only the Morts I can move. I can move the living as well, a gift given me directly, to fulfill my purpose. And you," he said, "are meant to join the Cruor. I am to help you achieve that."

The Cruor. The ones who fed on the blood of humans. Ophelia had seen things as a small child, though, as she'd grown older, she'd always imagined she'd confused reality with her mother's stories. Stories that had kept her up some nights, terrorizing her with nightmares to the point her father eventually insisted the fairytales come to an end. That night, her parents argued in living room, and Ophelia listened by her bedroom door.

'I'm preparing 'er,' Ophelia's mother had said to him crossly.

'Ye are *scaring* 'er,' he said. 'What is the point of all we 'ave accomplished if ye still cling to that world, Eleanor?'

'She needs to know.'

Ophelia's mother had always been firm. In most families Ophelia knew, a woman would never question her husband's wishes, but their family was different. Ophelia's mother was often the one to make the final judgment calls in their house.

"Leave it alone, Eleanor. At least until she's older."

They'd settled on that, but Ophelia never forgot the haunting tales of the savage the Cruor had wreaked.

Deep down, she'd always known her mother's stories were more than just fairytales.

"If I am to become one of the Cruor, then my mother must have been Ankou and Strigoi, yes? Clearly she was not one of the Chibold."

Ethan rubbed his hand over the stubble that darkened his jaw. "Yes. Her dual-bred nature would have allowed her to walk in the sun undetected."

"That won't be possible for me if I do as ye say I must, will it?"

Ethan leveled his gaze at her. "It is not an ideal situation, but—"

"It is a *terror*. And ye are saying I am destined to become one of them? To become the enemy of my own family?"

"You wouldn't be the enemy."

"Of course not," Ophelia said bitterly. "Ye can't be an enemy to the dead!"

"Ophelia . . . " he said gently, but she spun around where she sat and squeezed her eyes against the tears. "That's not what I meant."

Her chest tightened, and she fought back the sobs. She needed to pull herself together. Needed to get away from here, away from Ethan, away from this 'calling' that would dare ask this of her. Ask her to become *Cruor*. If there was a higher power, it would not want another one of *them* walking this earth.

"Becoming Cruor is your only way to gain acceptance to the Maltorim," Ethan said. His tone was almost pleading.

Ophelia crossed her arms in disgust, shaking her head. She need hear no more. Mother had said the Maltorim were a council of elementals chosen to carry out the wishes of the Universe, but since they had become an entity primarily ruled by Cruor, they had used their power to serve themselves alone and to execute anyone who stood in their way.

"Ye are suggesting I join the evil ones. No, Ethan. I shall never do such a thing. Never."

"Never?" Ethan's brow furrowed. "You don't have much choice, unless you intend to suffer. You're destined to join them. If you do not, they will one day overtake the earth. Many innocent people will die. You can prevent that from happening by joining the Maltorim and helping the girl who will one day be sent there to bring forth change."

"I 'ave a choice," Ophelia said. "Everyone 'as a choice."

"So your choice is what? To walk away? To allow thousands to die? For what? So that you can return to a life of scrubbing floors and delivering messages in the dead of night?" His fists clenched at his side. "I am not asking to behave as they behave, Ophelia. I'm only asking you walk among them so you can save the human girl who can rid of them completely."

Ophelia hurriedly buttoned up her gown. "Thank ye for helping with the sting," she said. "Please, excuse me. I 'ave a long way to travel come sunrise. I need my rest."

Part of her wished to leave immediately, but she sensed she was at least a bit safer with this man, in this cabin, than she would be in the woods alone at night with no idea where she was or which way to go. Surely, though, he hadn't really taken her to Damascus? Come morning, she would circle outward, just as her father had taught her back home when they were trying to find something lost. Eventually she would fall upon the forest and find the trail Ethan had abducted her from.

Ophelia stood and walked purposefully over to the cot beside the cabin window and blew out the candle on the bedside table. Though she could feel Ethan's gaze following her, he maintained his silence as she climbed under the woolen blanket and rolled onto her side to stare out the window into the night sky.

The stars looked different here. Brighter. Unobstructed by the clouds that muted them back home. The grass here was so dry, so silvered and patchy in a way that indicated they couldn't be anywhere near the usual greenery from whence they'd come.

Were they really in Damascus?

Silly, she chided herself. *Silly to believe* any *of this!*

She sighed and flipped onto her back and closed her eyes, Ethan's gaze still burning into her senses. In her mind's eye, she could visualize him sitting in the chair by the fire, resting forward with his hands clasped between his knees, staring at her through the rogue tumble of his dark chestnut hair. The sheen of his tanned skin in the firelight, and the sparks of gold in his earthy-brown eyes.

Her breathing was shallow, and she hoped the rise and fall of her chest was hidden well beneath the blanket. The last thing she needed was him to think he had any power over her or effect on her emotions, that he was what she was thinking of as she lie in bed. Should he realize that, he might be too quick to attempt to manipulate her.

"It won't go away," Ethan said finally, his voice cutting through every emotion she was fighting to deny. "The burning will return. It will get worse. And it will not stop until you've honored your calling."

She would *not* listen to him. She would release every idea he had suggested. Her mother was alive—that she needed to believe—and she could not waste time here playing these games with this strange man. If she didn't at least try to find her mother, she would spend the rest of her life wondering, "*What if?*"

In the past, Ophelia had been one to waver in her beliefs, to be easily swayed into changing her thinking, but right now, her life and future were on the line. If she had to fight who she was in order to stay true to herself, then she would welcome such a contradiction.

DAMASCUS, 1808

OPHELIA SAT up in bed and rubbed the sleep from her eyes. The one small window in the cabin, located right beside her bed, was covered with a wool blanket, but the morning light that slanted in had roused her awake. The mark along her neck radiated a warm tingle, a reminder of the night before. A reminder, also, of the way Ethan's fingers had so delicately brushed her skin there as he'd unbuttoned her gown.

"Good morning, Ophelia."

At the sound of Ethan's voice, the whole of the situation came rushing back to her. Her gaze darted to the fireplace. He was still sitting in the same place, staring into the crackle of the fire.

"Is it?" she snapped.

There was nothing good about this morning. Ophelia reached to pull the blanket away from the window, to peek outside, but as soon as the light cut into the room, something thumped behind her.

Ophelia's gaze averted to the broad-shouldered man now standing behind her. The morning light revealed translucent, butterfly-like wings that stretched from his back to up above his head and down to the floor.

The sheer wings, however, were not beautiful as she'd imagined. Instead they were amniotic, like the filmy membrane that clung to animals during birth, with black veins spreading throughout like bloodshot eyes.

Ophelia gasped a small intake of air, and a bit of peace settled over her. At the very least, he was what he claimed.

"Close it." His tone was stern but his dark eyes conveyed . . . panic? Once she'd honored his request, he eased back into his chair. "Please keep the blanket up until nightfall."

"Are ye afraid of being seen for what ye really are?" Ophelia asked.

In that moment, Ethan's expression relaxed. Was it her wide-eyed gaze that softened him? Or perhaps the innocent note of questioning in her voice?

Part of Ophelia hoped his wings *would* be seen—that someone would happen upon their cabin and rescue her. The other part of her, however, could not deny her heart's strange desire to stay. Her father would have scolded her to make up her mind. She had, though. Ethan left her curious, to say the least. He made her cheeks warm when he was near and often left her fighting off the urge to giggle. She could slap herself for being so childishly infatuated with him, but ultimately she could not resist. Her only doubt now was whether she'd become sure of something that would only lead her to tragedy.

Regardless, she couldn't go anywhere until she did something about the burning mark of the serpent. She would allow her mind and heart to debate later.

Ethan sighed, lifting his gaze to her. "Direct sunlight does more than reveal our kind. It also alters our physical form. When you accept your calling, you will have to avoid the light as well."

The stories rushed back into Ophelia's mind: the sun could shrink the Ankou over time, reducing them to little more than the size of a dragonfly.

"My mother," Ophelia said, "walked in the sun many times."

"She was part Strigoi. This is why the Maltorim want the dual-natured dead. With twice the abilities and half the weaknesses, they are seen as a threat."

"Then why do they need our assistance?"

"They are fewer in number," Ethan said, "and the abilities they have are weaker than those of the purebreds."

"And we can assist by becoming purebreds ourselves?"

"That's the idea."

Quite done entertaining Ethan's fairytales, Ophelia rose and made the bed.

"Breakfast?" she asked.

When he didn't respond, she turned toward him, catching the tender expression writ in his handsome features. He cleared his throat and nodded toward the kitchenette.

"We're stuck 'ere till night, then, are we?" she asked as she rummaged through the cabinets.

"Mmm-hmm."

The deep rumble of his voice gave Ophelia a pleasant shudder that she immediately sought to repress. This was a man who had snatched her from her safe, if miserable, life and taken her thousands of miles away. She needed to think of something else.

Breakfast. There must be something here.

Empty mason jars crammed the cabinets and, as she shuffled them about, the glass clinked together. Ethan placed one hand on the counter beside her, and as he reached over her shoulder to sweep the jars aside, his chest pressed against her back. The heat radiating from his body warmed her from her neck to the space behind her weakened knees.

This was completely inappropriate, and yet her body was eager for the connection. She fought the urge to lean back against him, to warm herself against the cabin's chill. Or, perhaps, her desire for his touch was something more. She swallowed.

"Allow me," he said, leaning down to whisper warmly against her ear.

His aroma of cloves heightened her senses, and she stiffened, steeling herself against the attraction. "What would ye prefer to eat?" she asked.

He reached past her, and, from behind the rows of jars, deep in the back of the cabinets, he grabbed a jar of preserves. He placed it on the counter beside the bread.

"Thank ye," she whispered.

He froze, staring tenderly into her eyes, his gaze touching every part of her face. Boldly, she stared back. The energy that had risen up between them refused to let her go. After a long moment, Ethan looked away, toward the door, and stepped back.

"Hungry?" he asked.

Ophelia turned to the counter and forced her attention to the food, allowing Ethan his chance to escape whatever had just happened between them. Her heart fluttered like a hummingbird inside her chest. She dipped a spoon into the preserves to taste how fresh they were. It was a blackberry spread, sweet with a little tang, just the way her father had always liked.

She peeked over her shoulder at Ethan, only to find him watching her intently.

"I would hate me if I were you," he said.

She smiled to herself and kept herself busy by examining the bread. "I would never make it so easy."

"How can you be so forgiving?" His serious tone held steadfast.

Ophelia chewed her lip. What was she to tell him? That despite it all, he had shown her more kindness than any man before? That she could not fault him for honoring something he believed in, even if she herself still failed to feel the same?

That no matter what their situation might be, she simply could not help the way she felt about him . . . this attraction . . . much less fight it?

She hadn't even considered forgiveness.

"It's easier this way," she said finally.

She closed her eyes to the silence for a long time, her mind overwhelmed. Her thoughts until now were to get home. Which was where, exactly? Lady Karina's estate? Paxton? Britain? Did she still want to return? No, she decided, she did not. Nor did she want to do what the Universe had called her to do. What she wanted was to stay here, in this in-between, in this sensation of falling with Ethan, in these moments where she felt breathless and her heart fluttered in her chest.

Behind her, Ethan was mumbling to himself, and she strained to hear the words of the familiar cadence.

" . . . winter bound her veins; so grows both stream and source of price, that lately fettered were with ice. So naked trees . . . "

" . . . get crisped 'eads," Ophelia said, still focused on the meal preparation. "And colored coats the roughest meads."

Ethan had gone silent, and Ophelia turned toward him.

"And all that vigor, youth, and spright . . . " she said, and as she continued, he joined in, " . . . that are but looked on by his light."

Their gaze lingered on one another, Ethan's chest void of the movement that comes with breathing. A watery-glaze filmed his deep brown eyes, and the fire shimmered against the golden hues.

At last, he released the air from his lungs and shook his head. "You are a maid, and yet you recite Benjamin Johnson as though you were a scholar."

"I am more than what defines me," she said. "Aren't we all?"

"Not all of us. Not me."

Ophelia took the prepared plate of food for them to share

and lowered herself to Ethan's side by the fire. "I don't believe that one bit."

"You don't have to."

Ophelia placed her hand on his. "We are all more, when we allow ourselves to be."

Ethan pulled his hand back and indicated the serpent's mark on Ophelia's neck. "How is the pain?"

She sighed. How foolish she had been to expect this man to open up to her. "The sting is returning."

He nudged the dish from last night toward her. "There's not much left."

With one finger, she tugged the dish closer. A thin film of red remained at the bottom of the dish. "What is it?"

"Cruor blood," he said. "To ease the sting completely, that is the blood you need flowing through your own veins."

"And for ye?" she asked. "It'd been the blood of the Ankou?"

"For me it had been nothing. I did not resist my calling."

"Whose blood is this?"

"Don't let it concern you."

Ophelia remained firmly still. "Tell me."

Ethan let out of a heavy breath. "The rule of the hunter is to never waste your kill. It's not a sport. It's a necessity."

Ophelia crossed her arms and leveled her gaze at him. "So ye just killed some man, then? Ethan—"

"Some *man?*" His brow furrowed, and his expression grew dark. "You know as well as I what the Cruor are. I would hardly call him a man. I did what I had to do. Someday, so will you."

So Ophelia was to become something seen as less than human? She closed her eyes for a moment, her thoughts swimming through her options. "If I were to do this—and I'm not saying I will—what would I need to do?"

The start of a smile played at the corner of his mouth.

"You will do it. You know you must, and more than that, I believe you want to."

She scowled at his amusement. "Why would I want to?"

"To honor your mother. This would be your chance to save many of her kind."

"But kill how many 'umans in the process? 'ow is that any better?"

"There are other ways to hunt, if that is all that holds you back."

No, it wasn't all that held her back. Ethan wasn't telling her anything she didn't already know. She could hunt deer or some other wildlife. It's not as though she'd never hunted before. But to hunt as a Cruor . . . ? She shook the thought away.

"Ye haven't answered what I've asked, Sir Ethan," she said dryly. "What is it I'm expected to do in all of this?"

"Make a trade with one of the Cruor." The timbre of his voice sparked every nerve along her spine.

Ophelia narrowed her eyes, her attraction for him wisely retreating to the far corners of her mind. "What kind of trade?"

"In exchange for turning you Cruor, I will offer the one who changes you the gift of sun magic. They will also have the gift of feeding on your blood, something that usually requires hunting an unwilling participant. You would be different."

"Excuse me?" Ophelia leaned away. "I assure ye, I am no willing participant."

"They will need to bite you for you to be turned. And if we don't want them to kill you completely, we'll have to offer something in return. I can grant them the ability to walk in sunlight."

"Wouldn't their bloodlust prevent that from ever 'appening."

"I know someone," he said, placing his hand over hers. "She may accept the offer."

Ophelia stared down at his hand resting on her own, and her heart thumped in her chest with a sudden pressure that left her breathless. Ethan followed her gaze and slowly eased his hand away. He didn't return his gaze to hers—only stared at the fire, the crackling glow illuminating his bronze skin and firm jaw.

"I'm sorry," he said finally. "I should never lose focus, especially not with you. Are you prepared to do what needs to be done?"

"I am not sure I want to give any Cruor that kind of power," she said, thinking of her mother's stories once more. Visions of her father's dead body flashed through her mind, and a realization hit her stomach with a sudden cold. Sharp, triangular scabs on her father's jugular. It'd been them, hadn't it? Not a robbery. That's why nothing had been missing. "And then what? I become one of them—what purpose is there?"

"Then we will find a way to get you into the Maltorim, where you will wait for a girl."

"Right. A girl, then. Will any girl do, or might ye have someone particular in mind? I am sure I can round up something for ye without all this trouble."

"You know full well what I mean. You will know the girl when you see her, and only you will know."

The more he spoke, the more impossible this task appeared. And that is when it occurred to her: She was considering the transformation—more so than she like to would admit. But how much of that was resignation or disbelief? The whole ordeal still carried the haze of a dream. And here she was with a man she was oddly drawn to and at the same time should probably be trying to escape.

"When would this occur?" she asked finally.

Ethan shook his head. "I can't answer that."

"Can't?" Ophelia throat pinched and tears stung in her eyes. "Or won't?"

His eyes searched hers, and a trembling started at her core. He didn't respond.

"Will ye come with me?" she asked quietly.

His gaze lowered. "I have to do what I'm called for. I need to know you will do the same."

She squeezed her eyes shut for a moment and replayed everything through her mind once more. Her parents would never want this. Never. But, at the same time, wouldn't they be proud if they knew she'd sacrificed herself to save many? That was what she admired in Ethan, even if his selflessness stood between anything they might have between them.

"I will do my best," she promised. But still she was unsure she could go through with it.

With that, Ethan stood to tend the fire, his back to her as silence recaptured the room.

FROM DAMASCUS TO GEORGIA, 1808

NIGHT CREPT OVER DAMASCUS. After treating the rapidly warming serpent mark with more Cruor blood, Ophelia spun toward the open door. Ethan sat between the frame, his strong shoulders resting back, his face turned to the field where a small red fox burrowed in the dirt. The night breeze wisped through his hair. She set the blankets on the end of the bed and walked over.

"Is it far?" she asked.

"No." He cleared his throat but didn't look up at her. "Sorry. For a human, it's very far, but it won't be for us."

Ophelia bunched her fingers together in front of her stomach. "Same as we got 'ere then?"

"Yes."

She stepped around, outside, and kneeled in the grass across from him, resting her hands in her lap. "Ethan, if something is wrong . . . "

"I'd tell you," he replied, lifting his gaze from a long piece of grass he'd been slipping between his fingers. Moonlight paled his tan complexion and darkened the shade of his jaw, making him appear more defeated than he had hours ago.

"The Cruor I mentioned earlier is in the Americas. She's not expecting us."

"But I thought—"

"Please trust me." He stood and dusted off his pants, then leaned his shoulder against the doorjamb.

She tried for a smile and busied herself attempting to prop up a wildflower that was wilting among the yellow grass.

When she looked up, Ethan's expression was gentle. His gaze moved from the small flower to her eyes. There was a brief moment where she wondered if he, like Lady Karina, found her bright, ice-blue eyes alarming. But his express was soft, and her fears quickly melted. He walked behind her, crouched down, and covered her hand with his, his fingertips touching the flower. It revived before her very eyes, and Ophelia leaned her head against Ethan's shoulder as she stared at the flower in awe.

"Beautiful," she whispered, wishing she had been destined to be one of the Ankou—to be one of the elementals who revived life and put an end to evil, rather than bring death.

She told him as much.

He sat back, and she turned around to face him. He was standing now, holding his hand out to her.

"Come with me," he said.

He took her hand and they fell through darkness just as they had when he'd taken her to the cabin. When she could see again, her stomach suddenly jolted. She hunched forward, heaving, but this time she did not vomit. She held her midsection until the feeling passed, then dried the moisture from her eyes.

Ethan smoothed his hand across her shoulder blades. "Traveling will get easier with time. By your third or fourth time you shouldn't feel anything."

"Why does this keep happening?" she demanded. She could hardly think straight.

"When we travel this way, we are in the *in-between*. You are suspended from such things as time and space and then thrust immediately back into it. Your system is forced to catch up instantly on arrival. If not for the magic the Ankou are granted, it could kill you."

Ophelia sighed, nodding. "Where are we?"

Ethan turned her toward a small house and pressed his fingers to his lips.

He led her along the outer walls of the house until they reached a window. Inside, a man and a woman held each other, crying. Ophelia peered around the room, trying to make sense of what she was searching for. She found her answer on the floor. A young man sat, collapsed to his knees, covered in blood.

"What 'appened?" Ophelia whispered.

"The young man just watched his comrades kill his sister." Ethan's voice was tight and his tone clipped. "He was unable to act to save her. He's returned home to tell their parents."

Ophelia backed away, shaking her head. When Ethan approached, she pounded her fist against his chest. "Why would ye show me such a thing?"

Ethan didn't move, even as Ophelia tried once again to push him away. "The young girl who lost her life was a dual-breed. She was only killed because of what she is, and for no greater reason. This . . . this is what we're fighting for. It is not that I want you in harm's way, or that I wish for you to become a creature you detest. If I could do this for you, protect you from your calling, I would. But I cannot let my feelings for you sway our responsibility. I am confident you are capable, that you can do this to save the innocents in this world."

Though Ophelia tried, she could not summon a response. She covered her mouth with hand, her entire body trembling. Could she live with herself, knowing all this, if she didn't try to help?

They walked away from the house silently and stopped

when they reached a small brook. Ethan leaned in to whisper against her ear. "We are destined for good. Remember that life sometimes must run its course, and all things must one day die. Some of us sooner than others."

She nodded quietly, lifting her lashes until her gaze met his. He kept his attention steady on her as her hand slipped gently into his, and her heart pattered quicker in response. He pulled her to him as though she were weightless, as though the earth had reversed its gravity.

His other hand came to rest on the small of her back, and he tilted his face, his nose grazing hers. "This—" His Adam's apple bobbed. "This isn't good for either of us."

"I don't care," she said, staring at his lips as her free hand slid up to the firm curve of his shoulder. "Ethan . . . "

She should not trust these feelings. She'd never been a good judge of character, and for that knowledge she'd always stayed away from men. Yet in Ethan's arms, Ophelia felt small in size but tremendous in devotion.

He closed his eyes and breathed. "You smell like rain and strawberries."

She inhaled slowly, taking in his own familiar scent of cloves. Their bodies swayed in a way that made her wonder if her legs had gone numb, and it felt as though his touch alone held her up.

Ethan swept his thumb over the bridge over her nose, tracing her freckles from there and across her cheekbones. His tender gaze focused on hers. "I'm going to kiss you now . . . if that's all right."

Ethan's words hung in the air as her thoughts rushed by. No one had ever asked her permission before. While staying with Lady Karina, she'd had to fight off a few vile men who expected quite a bit more from the maids than Ophelia was willing to offer. Lady Karina's brother had been one of them.

Stupid girl, he'd said when she rejected him. *You'd only be so lucky.*

"Ophelia?"

"Yes," she said, but her reply came too late.

He shook his head. "I don't know what I was thinking."

He smiled down at her then, and the world around them shifted. The air vibrated, creating a haze of images, and then there was total darkness and the feeling they were falling. Falling through space, falling together.

They came out of the darkness just a few feet away from the woods. The air tasted of dirt and pine, and the night birds chirped from somewhere above. A queasiness washed through her, making her shiver, and she grabbed her stomach.

"Welcome to Savannah," Ethan said. He grabbed her at the elbow, helping to keep her steady.

The nausea passed more quickly this time than the times before and, relieved, she smiled at Ethan. In the dark, she could barely make out the smile he gave in return, but she knew it was not one of happiness.

"What's wrong?"

He glanced into the woods behind her. "Maybe we shouldn't do this."

"What do ye mean? We must." He'd spent all that time convincing her, and now, as she made peace with the idea—as much as she could—he expressed doubts? "Ye said there was no other way."

"We'll find one."

Ophelia stepped back, crossing her arms. "What aren't ye telling me?"

He closed the distance between them once more. "Forgive me, Ophelia. I can't do this to you. I thought I could, but I would forever regret putting you in such danger. There is no one less deserving of such a bleak future."

"Where is the man of such devotion who was with me only hours ago? The man so willing of sacrifice?"

"You cannot compare sacrificing oneself to sacrificing another."

"Don't tell me the cause is now lost on ye. This is not about me alone; there are thousands of dual-breeds facing execution."

"Or it could be your life that is lost. Perhaps . . . " He closed his eyes a long moment before opening them again. "Perhaps I was devoted to the wrong things."

"Ye don't believe that," Ophelia said sharply. "Why is this coming up now? Ye said this Cruor would be receptive."

"She will be. Eventually . . . " His gaze refocused on her. "I don't exactly know her, only what my guardian told me of her when explaining what my calling would entail. I was told she would be receptive if she would hear what I have to say first."

"If?"

"Before she kills us. A chance I cannot take with you."

Ophelia searched his eyes, finding nothing more than the empty weight of hopelessness. How could she put her own, single life above everyone else's? For once, she understood where Ethan had been coming from. She needed to do this for her mother. She needed to do this for . . . everyone.

"We must, mustn't we?" she asked, but it wasn't really a question. This wasn't a matter of fate anymore.

"Everyone has a choice," he said gravely. "You still believe that, do you not?"

"I do," she said. "And this one is mine."

Breathing in a focused breath, she turned away and walked toward the trail into the woods. She couldn't very well go back to Lady Karina's estate now. She couldn't turn away from what had been done to her mother. Maybe her father had been right. She could be more than a servant.

Ethan's heavy boots crunched the branches along the trail behind her. Moonlight pierced through the winter-bare canopy above. The patchy night sky provided just enough light for Ophelia to make her way along the path, but she knew from her mother's stories that the light of the moon was as bright as the sun to Ethan. Neither said another word until they reached a break in the path.

"Her camp is on the other side of the clearing," Ethan said.

"She's turned anyone before?"

Ethan's expression darkened. "No."

Ophelia gave a resolute nod. "Well, that certainly is good to know. What do we do now?"

"Stay behind me. It's best I approach her first."

The bushes rustled behind them, and Ophelia spun around. A petite girl, not much older than sixteen, stood on the path only a couple of feet away. Her oil-black hair tumbled around her shoulders. Moonlight glinted off the dark locks that framed her face. Her pale skin did not have the healthy glow of a well-fed Cruor. Instead, it was more alabaster white, pasty and nearly translucent. Only her cornflower blue eyes held any sign of life.

She snapped out her fangs and hissed, crouching down.

Ophelia gasped and stepped back, Ethan taking a protective stance in front of her.

"Sara?" he asked, edging Ophelia further away.

In a blur of movement, the girl was standing inches from him, her face level with his chest, but her gaze locked on his eyes. "Don't. Call. Me. Sara."

He retreated another step, nearly tripping over Ophelia. Her elbow grazed a tree behind her, and she grabbed Ethan's shoulder to catch her balance.

In another flash of movement, Ophelia found herself pinned to the ground in the clearing. Damn to hell the inhuman speed of the Cruor. The Cruor-girl held Ophelia's wrists against the ground so tightly that her nails dug into her flesh. A bead of sweat rolled from her hair-line, cool against the heat of the serpent's mark. Ophelia pushed, but the girl didn't budge. She tried to twist away, but the girl's surprising weight kept Ophelia in place.

Ethan broke through the trees into the clearing. He scanned the area until his gaze landed on Ophelia with fear and realization. "Sara, wait!"

The Cruor screamed, snapping her attention to Ethan.

Ophelia took the moment of distraction to shove her arms forward with all her might. The girl tumbled off of her, and Ethan pounced on her before she could rise, pinning her to the ground just as she had held Ophelia in place.

"We're here to give you something," he said.

Their figures blurred, and then the Cruor had the upper hand once more. She sat straddled over Ethan, her tiny hand wrapped around his neck. Her fingernails dug deep, sinking into his skin.

Ophelia stepped forward. "Leave 'im alone."

"You came to *my* home," the girl said. "You do not tell *me* what to do."

"The man ye are about to kill can give ye the ability to walk in the sun."

"Impossible."

Ethan struggled under her grasp.

"Possible," he croaked.

"Lenore," the Cruor said. "My name is Lenore now." She released her grasp on Ethan's neck, and replaced the space on his throat with her boot. "Tell me why you are here."

Ophelia strode over. "Ye want to walk in the sun, it is 'is blood and magic ye need."

Lenore smirked, and swung her gaze toward Ophelia. "If I want his blood, I can just take it."

"It won't do ye any good if 'e doesn't give it to ye willingly," Ophelia said, remembering her mother's stories of the magic of the Ankou.

Lenore narrowed her eyes. "And why would he want to do that?"

"'e doesn't, I'll tell ye that. We need a bit of 'elp ourselves."

"You want to trade with one of the Cruor?" Lenore quirked one eyebrow. "Are you sure?"

"If you are willing to trade with one of the Ankou," Ethan said.

The moon glinted in his eyes, and Ophelia, coming undone by her stress, hid her smile with her hand. The Ankou, her mother had always said, could be a bit mischievous.

Lenore stood and allowed Ethan up from the ground. "I will keep the girl until your magic is proven."

Ethan glared at her. "No."

"No?" Lenore asked. "Then I will take both your lives now."

"And you will have gained nothing for it."

"I smell your desperation." Lenore sneered. "You need me more than I need you."

"Then stay with us," he offered. "You will have the protection of our home from the sun and easy accessibility to us if we are not true to our word."

"What do you want?"

"We need you to turn Ophelia."

Lenore laughed. She turned away, tilted her head toward the night sky, and laughed again. She flopped down into the grass, her laughter continuing to roll through her until blood dotted the corners of her eyes. "You couldn't possible mean this!"

The whole ordeal was unsettling.

Lenore inhaled deeply and sharpened her gaze on Ophelia.

"Sit," she said. "Tell me what brings you here. I love a good story."

They did, and soon an agreement was made. They would execute a ritual to transfer some of the Ankou's magic to Lenore. She would stay with them until morning, and if their promise held good, she would turn Ophelia.

44

HAVING RETURNED TO DAMASCUS, 1808

AFTER RETURNING to Ethan's cabin, Lenore ventured into the nearby village and lured a man back to their secluded field. Ophelia watched in horror as the Cruor-girl drained the poor man of his life.

Ethan eased her away from the curtain and guided her over to the fire. He tried to talk to her, but the agonized face of the dying young man burned into Ophelia's memory as she stared at the flames.

Shortly thereafter, Lenore strolled in with blood staining her mouth, cheeks, and chin.

"'ow could ye?" Ophelia demanded.

"What?" Lenore asked. Her eyes were brighter now, her skin no longer translucent but instead the smooth pallor of porcelain. "A girl's got to eat."

ONE OF THE final herbs needed to perform the sunlight magic grew in a large stretch of forest in Denmark, and because Ophelia didn't trust Lenore, she joined Ethan when he ventured out to collect the ingredient.

They paused just outside a wooded area. Ethan lifted a

finger to his lips, and Ophelia stood unmoving until his shoulders relaxed and he waved for her to follow.

"I want to show you something while we're here," he said, leading her through the thicket onto what was not quite a path.

When she hesitated, he stopped, reached back, and took her hand. There was security to be found there, with his strong hand wrapped around hers, his palm warm against her own, but still Ophelia's heart throbbed with anxiety.

"We are safe," he whispered. "There is something you must see."

Ethan crouched on the path and gently tugged Ophelia to his side. Peering through the breaks in the leaves of the underbrush, Ophelia spotted a small campfire and a tent. Two men—if they could be called such—sat by the fire. Both of them had graying skin and enlarged skulls. When the first man spoke to the other, his lips pulled back to reveal a mouth full of jagged, pointed teeth

Ethan slapped his hand to her mouth to cover her gasp. He shook his head, his deep brown eyes wide with warning. One of the . . . *things* . . . looked up from the flames and in their direction. She squeezed Ethan's hand and pressed her lips together in fear she would vomit.

Ethan encircled her with his strong arms, the last herb they'd set out to gather clutched in his right hand, and then they fell into the darkness once more, traveling through space with the images of those men and a thousand questions still rampaging through Ophelia's mind.

When Ophelia could see again, they were in front of their very normal cabin, her heart still pounding in her chest. Ethan's arms held her tighter.

"I apologize," he whispered.

"What—" Ophelia nearly choked on the word. "What were they?"

"Ankou," he said quietly.

"No," she said, pushing away from him. "They couldn't be."

"I told you before what happens when our kind are exposed to too much sunlight. Those men tried to reverse the sun's effect on them by drinking Strigoi blood."

"But they look nothing like ye."

Ethan's lips pressed in a grim line. "They will never again look like men. They will have to feed on Strigoi blood for the rest of their lives to maintain their current state. To stop now would bring an excruciating death."

Ophelia knew she shouldn't judge them for their appearance alone, though surely it was their carelessness that led them to their current state. Just the same, the sight of them had terrified her. And how did they acquire the Strigoi blood? Fearing the answer might make her sick, she couldn't even bring herself to ask.

"I should not have discouraged you earlier." Ethan took hold of her delicate hands. "There are consequences should you deny your calling. I showed you those men so that you would understand what I mean. I let my heart get in the way earlier, and for that I nearly failed as your guardian."

"Ye 'aven't failed me."

He lowered his watery gaze. "I will rob you of your life, or of your destiny. I fail you either way."

"Ethan—"

He cleared his throat. "Enough of that, now."

Ethan entered the cabin, but Ophelia remained outside for a few minutes trying to think of a way in which they would be free to explore their feelings for one another, but no amount of staring at the horizon provided answers. After she calmed her nerves, she followed him in and sat at the far corner of the room. Lenore raised an eyebrow, and Ophelia told her to stay away.

Lenore sneered. "Don't worry, princess, I've already eaten."

"That man," Ophelia said. "Perhaps 'e was somebody's son, somebody's 'usband or—"

"Or someone's rapist or murderer," Lenore interrupted, a tired note to her voice.

Ophelia glared at her and stepped closer to Ethan. He was so completely absorbed in his dishes and herbs that he didn't seem to hear a word.

"Let's get this over with," Lenore said, breezing past Ophelia to peer over his shoulder.

Now if Ophelia wanted to get away from the Cruor-girl, she would have to step away from Ethan as well. She crossed the room and sat on the edge of the cot.

"What is it?" Lenore asked, nudging his shoulder.

"Hmm?" He fidgeted with a few herbs and then glanced up. "Oh. Sun magic requires balance."

He pushed forward a dish filled with green, stringy leaves that smelled so strongly of dried apple Ophelia could taste it on the air. "Chamomile prepares the body for the magic and purifies your system."

The next dish he revealed held three cinnamon sticks. "Protection."

Two final dishes contained Acacia—also for protection—and patchouli for healthy growth. Ethan explained each was an herb of the sun that represented one of the elements.

"Healthy growth?" Lenore asked.

Ethan started emptying the herbs into a small pot. "Will help with your pallor. You'll appear more human. Though the herb may also encourage passionate love."

She huffed. "I'd have preferred to be taller."

Ophelia watched the two with growing fascination. "Where did ye learn all this?"

"My father," Ethan said. He scraped his hand over the shading of his jaw. "He owned several ancient ritual books. I'd read them with great interest as a child, but it wasn't until I joined the Ankou that I was able to utilize the information.

The Ankou all carry a unique magic, but that is also only as good as their knowledge."

"And ye are sure it will work?" Ophelia asked.

"Yes," he said. "I think."

Lenore scowled. "What do you mean, you think?"

"It should. However, I've never done this before."

She sat on the floor in front of the pot. Ophelia kept her place on the edge of the cot by the window, warily eyeing Ethan as he produced an English trade knife, not much unlike her father's knife—the one with the sturdy wood handle and the strong steel blade.

Ethan closed his eyes and dragged the blade across the inside of his palm. He squeezed his hand over the pot, dripping blood on the herbs.

"Do vita donum cruoris voluntas," he chanted. The blood kept coming, and Ophelia's stomach turned, her heart thundering in her chest. "Do vita donum cruoris voluntas."

Ophelia's mother had spoken Latin; Ethan was chanting that he was giving his blood willingly. The red liquid continued to run down his fingers and into the bowl. So much blood. Why wasn't he stopping? His hand shook and his skin paled. As the blood flowed, Ethan stumbled forward where he knelt, and had to catch himself on an arm that seemed to quiver under his own weight.

When Ophelia was about to intervene, Ethan finally stopped, clutching his other hand over the bleeding wound. She hurried over to the fireplace and grabbed the bowl of Cruor blood he'd used to help her earlier. She grabbed his hand and was about to try to heal the wound, but Ethan pulled free.

"It won't work," he said.

Using his knife, he cut a strip of fabric from one of the sheets and wrapped it three times around his palm. Ophelia tied the ends in a tight knot at the back of his hand. Why was Lenore just sitting there? Didn't she care? Ethan was doing this for her, too, and she just sat there wide-eyed and staring.

"I'm okay, Ophelia," Ethan said, touching her forearm.

Instead of returning to the bed, Ophelia sat at his side, glaring at the dark-haired woman on the other side of the pot. Ethan stirred the mixture with a ladle and continued with the second chant.

"Feras praesidium ab sol." At his side lay a small disk with the mark of the Sun goddess riding on her chariot. He grasped the chain and lowered the charm into the mixture as he continued his chant—the chant to infuse the herbs and Ankou blood with protection from the sun.

Outside, the wind pressed against the cabin, creaking the wooden walls and rattling the windows. The sky flashed, and the weight of a storm permeated the air inside the cabin— moist, heavy, cold. Ophelia's skin prickled, and she opened her mouth to speak, but she could find no words. Ethan and Lenore's attention stayed on the ritual, as though nothing unusual were happening, and unease tingled in Ophelia's lungs.

The door blew open, and a dead raven thudded on the doorstep. Ophelia jumped up and stepped back, the ominous feeling rushing into her stomach like dry sand.

"Stop," she said. "Something's wrong."

Ethan continued, a golden-white glow emanating from his skin.

"Ethan!" Ophelia grabbed his shoulder. The heat of his flesh burned her fingers, and she snapped her hand away. "Stop it. Stop, *please.*"

He ladled the mixture into a cup and handed it to Lenore, who immediately began to drink as his chanting carried on. The ground trembled and everything around them rattled— the plates and cups in the cabinets, the cot against the floor, the pot between them.

When Lenore finished, she put the necklace around her

neck and closed her eyes. A grimace overtook her features, and she grabbed her stomach.

"What 'ave ye done?"

Ethan shook his head, his gaze focused on nothing in particular. Finally, with another shake of his head, his gaze settled on Ophelia's with renewed clarity. "It's all right. She's changing, that is all. You will still need to undergo your own transformation, but Lenore cannot feed from you in her current state. She won't be able to control her urges."

Unable to control her urges? She keeled over and clutched her stomach, gasping for air, her face contorted in agony.

"What's going on?" Ophelia demanded.

He shook his head. "Not now."

She curled her fists at her side. Her heart pounded in her chest and anger churned her stomach. Something had overcome her, some outside pressure that seemed to tear every hidden emotion and doubt from her gut and force it to the surface. Her mind swam beneath the sudden confusion.

"What's in it for ye?" she demanded. "Tell me! Tell me why ye need me to do this so badly."

"Ophelia . . . I've told you this already. It is not for me. For me, I would never ask this of you. It is my duty to guide you toward your destiny, and it is your destiny to join the Maltorim. If either of us fails, the world as we know it will someday end, and everyone will suffer for it."

Lenore sputtered a cough, and Ophelia realized she was trying to laugh. The young Cruor wheezed, holding her hand tighter to her gut.

"If we don't obey our callings, the human race will one day become extinct. I will lose everyone I've ever loved, including—" His jaw clenched. "You have to—"

She wanted to push away her unreasonable emotions but her words betrayed her.

"That's what this is about?" She glared at him. "About ye?

About who *ye* will lose? What about me? Who is it ye are so afraid of losing?"

"Now?" he asked wearily. "You, Ophelia. This is not just about me. The mark of the serpent will kill you if you don't do as you are called. Maybe, somehow, the Universe might find someone to replace you on your journey if you don' survive. But, to me, you cannot be replaced."

The sentiment slammed into Ophelia, but she couldn't talk to him about this with Lenore writhing on the ground and all the ruckus in the room that he seemed to so easily ignore.

Ophelia looked again to the open door, to the dead bird, then up to the horizon. The sun was just about to break day. Ethan should have moved to shut the door, or cover the windows, but his silence thrummed at the back of her head.

In the distance, her mother was standing in the tall grass.

DAMASCUS, 1808

OPHELIA STEPPED OUTSIDE, squinting into the distance. Images of her childhood flashed through her mind: her mother tending to her skinned knees, her mother's lips on her hairline as she burned with fever, her mother telling stories while they sat knitting by the fire, and those gentle, wordless corrections each time Ophelia's needles faltered.

The whole world seemed to be still at that moment, weightless, drenched in the early-morning haze. Tears burned her eyes and blurred her vision. Her mother *was* still alive. Ophelia's heart thundered.

Ethan walked up behind her and placed his hand on her shoulder. "That's not your mother."

She turned. There were sheets now on the window. Lenore's hair, damp with sweat, coiled against the cot's pillow like dead river-snakes. Ophelia forced her gaze to Ethan, unwilling to allow any sympathies for the Cruor-girl to play over her heart.

"I'd know my mother if I saw 'er," she said. "And that is 'er."

"It's a shifter, Ophelia."

"Shifters cannot take the form of a 'uman." Wasn't that how the stories had gone?

"Times are changing."

"It is my mother," Ophelia persisted.

It *was* her, wasn't it? It had to be. Ophelia needed, more than anything, to believe this. This was the hope she'd held on to, the hope that kept her alive. Ethan could be right . . . but he could also be wrong. She couldn't risk not finding out for sure.

The sun was rising fast on the horizon. Its rays stretched across the field, illuminating Ethan's translucent Ankou wings. The black veins shimmered out past his shoulders and nearly all the way down to his ankles. He stepped back into the shadows.

"Please, Ophelia. Come inside."

As Ophelia started to pull the door closed, she kept her eyes to the floor, unable to settle her gaze on Ethan's furrowed brow and pleading eyes. "I must go to her."

The door clicked shut.

Though she feared Ethan was right, she would never forgive herself if she didn't take the chance. She could follow cautiously, get close enough to at least find out for sure. She *needed* to do this. Her mother—if it was her—might have answers. For starters, how had her mother gotten here? How could she have known where Ophelia was? Why come to her now?

Older questions—ones that had driven Ophelia's very existence in recent years—overwhelmed the newer ones. Where had her mother been all this time? Who killed Ophelia's father? Would her mother know a way to stop the burn of the serpent's mark without joining the darkness of the Cruor?

That was the idea that carried her forward, moving her through the field of tall grass. She could not have stayed back even if she'd wanted to.

The skirt of her mother's dress brushed the blades of the meadow in the breeze. She smiled softly and gave a gentle wave. Ophelia lifted her skirts and set off, at first walking. But as she got closer, as her certainty grew that it was her mother, she picked up her pace. She walked faster and faster until she was running across the field, until she neared the forest, neared the small grove along the edges that sprouted olive and lemon trees from the ground.

Her mother turned and started to walk away.

Why would she come all this way to leave me now? What stopped her from coming to the cabin?

Somewhere deep in Ophelia's gut came the urge to dart back to the cabin. But a voice, too much like her own, prodded at her mind. *Don't let fear stand in your way.* As much as she wanted to, she could not defy that voice. Ophelia could not turn back now.

"Wait!" she called.

Her mother walked into the grove and didn't turn back. The trees obstructed Ophelia's view.

Didn't she see Ophelia trying to catch up? Was she trying to show her something? Had the time away somehow . . . *changed* . . . her mother? If her mother needed help and Ophelia gave up now, she would never forgive herself. She ran harder until she breached the woods. Her mother's silhouette glided between the trees.

"Mother?"

The woman looked over her shoulder with a smile, but continued on her path.

Ophelia was compelled to chase. Dread, fear, warning— all these things washed through her, but a small flicker of hope with a mind all its own pushed her onward. Twenty meters into the woods, she caught up with the woman and found her leaning against a tree, crying.

"Why didn't ye wait for me?"

As Ophelia approached, her mother sobbed harder. With

her heart in her throat, Ophelia gently rested her hand on her mother's back. The woman turned around, grinning, laughing, and Ophelia stepped back. Her heart sank into her stomach, cold as ice and heavy with dread.

A man's voice cackled from her mother's mouth.

The woman's thin nose stretched, and her lips peeled back to reveal pink gums and blocky teeth. Every feature contorted until there was no trace of her mother's face remaining in the man's features. His shoulders broadened, and Ophelia gaze locked on his as his height stretched to tower a good head above her own.

"Robert." Ophelia could barely choke out his name. In the shadows, his strawberry-blond hair was more auburn, but she was certain it was him.

"Lovely to see you, too," Lady Katrina's brother replied. He grabbed her hand and kissed it roughly. "You're just as foolish as your father."

Ophelia snapped her hand back. "What do ye know about my father?"

Robert laughed. "Come now. Isn't the 'what' the whole reason you came to work for my sister in the first place? I'll save you the effort, fair Ophelia. There's nothing more to find."

"Ye killed 'er."

"The honor was not mine." Robert's grin stretched tighter. "Your father, however, proved to be quite the problem following her death. You really should have learned something from him. It's best to mind your own business."

"And what business is my family to ye?"

"Your mother was an abomination," said the man who had traveled all the way here in the time only an Ankou could have. A man who then shifted before Ophelia's very eyes. Did that not make him a dual-breed himself?

"Curious choice of words," Ophelia said, her voice shaking. "Ye are every bit a mutt as she."

His lips pursed. His brow furled over glowering eyes. "I agree with the Maltorim's orders. The impure are the real danger, to the humans *and* to the elemental races."

The boiling in her stomach rose to her chest. She chewed on her cheek and swallowed hard to hold her anger down.

"If there is blame to place, it's with the man who brought you here." Robert flicked a blade from its sheath in his pocket. The sun glinted off the steel as he shuffled toward her. "I would have liked to keep you, of course, but I must honor my duties."

"And she must honor hers." The voice came from behind Ophelia, sharp and yet feminine.

Lenore.

In one swift blurring arch of color, Lenore lunged at Robert and pinned him to the ground, digging her nails into his wrists until he dropped the blade. But Robert shifted again, his form growing too large for Lenore to keep a good grip. His clothes tore and fell from his body. Stripes ripped across his back, arms, and legs, and hair burst through the skin on his face. His skull and jaw distorted, his features more feline than man.

A tiger now stood before Ophelia and Lenore, teeth bared. A low growl rumbled from his chest as he backed away, fear flickering in his eyes before he turned and bounded off through the woods.

Gone. Just like that. She peered around, expecting to see a flash of him the underbrush or bounding toward them once again.

Lenore turned toward Ophelia, her fangs still fully extended, puffing out her mouth. "You all right?"

"Yes." Ophelia couldn't stop shaking. A heavy breeze rushed a fresh waft of lemon and olive toward her, and she nearly gagged on the scent as she tried to fight back her tears. "No. I—I don't know."

The young Cruor's fangs retracted with a snap. "He's been

injured. He won't fight me like that, not unless he's a damn fool."

"Sure is," Ophelia muttered, and Lenore laughed.

The humor didn't reach Ophelia though. She couldn't shake the feeling he was still watching, waiting for an opportunity to attack. Lenore, however, seemed at ease.

"He hates himself, you know." Her expression relaxed into something more human. "He couldn't control his shifting. He couldn't fight becoming something he didn't wish to be."

"That's why 'e ran off?" Ophelia asked. "Instead of . . . of . . ."

"Are you disappointed?" Lenore arched her eyebrow, smirking. How could she be so candid at a time like this? She nodded toward the path. "Come. Let's get you back to the cabin."

Once Ophelia was certain they were safe, new concerns tumbled into her mind. Ethan has been right. It hadn't been her mother. How had Ophelia been fooled, but Ethan had known? And if Robert was one of the Strigoi, how many secrets had her mother kept?

Her mother had always said that the Strigoi were honorable, but clearly Robert was not. Had her mother told her those stories in hopes of preparing Ophelia, should she ever be pulled into this world? If so, why hadn't she been completely forthright?

Perhaps Mother had hoped it would never really come to this.

Now she would never know, and she needed to accept it was no longer safe for her to entertain her childish fantasies of reuniting with her mother. Her mother gone. Truly and forever.

Ophelia had always thought accepting her mother's death would end all purpose in her life. That, without her mother, there would be nothing worth living for. Ethan changed all that. Ophelia would go through with the transformation and live her life with this new purpose of helping some girl she didn't know. She would do it in memory of those she had loved—those who had been stolen from this world far too soon.

DAMASCUS, 1808

AFTER PROMISING to return in the evening to prepare for Ophelia's transformation, Lenore left for the day. When the cabin door fell shut behind the Cruor, Ophelia turned to Ethan, her hurt and anger rushing through her in a violent upsurge.

"Why?" She lunged toward him and pounded her fist against his chest. "Why didn't ye tell me it was him?"

He grabbed her wrist and pulled her closer. Ophelia still pushed, wishing to get away from him and to hurt him at the same time.

"Please, Ophelia," Ethan whispered, and she froze at the pained tone in his voice. His eyes were moist and his expressed strained. "I wanted to come for you."

Wanted to? She shook her head. No words were worthy of the moment. All she could do was stand there, searching his eyes for answers to the questions that swarmed through her mind.

Ophelia swallowed around the tightness in her throat. The hurt and anger threatened to rush back. "Go on."

"I told you not to go," he said. "If I'd stopped you from

going, would you have ever forgiven me? Would you have ever trusted me enough to continue with what needed to be done?"

She bit her lip, but there was nothing she could say. She couldn't trust him any more for allowing her to leave than she would have if he'd stopped her from leaving. And she couldn't trust herself. She'd known, somewhere deep down, that her mother was dead. She'd known, yet she'd allowed herself to be fooled, all because of her childish desire to believe her mother was still alive.

Her heart longed to forgive him, but she could not push aside the feelings of abandonment. Her parents had kept the truth from her, and it left her helpless. How could Ethan do the same? Why hadn't he warned her of these things sooner?

"Ye could have tried 'arder to stop me."

"How?" His fists clenched at his side. "By grabbing you and dragging you back inside?"

She shook her head, and unease twisted in her stomach. Was he right—that she would not have listened to him anyway?

"It would have been worth it," Ethan said, his voice dropping into tones of defeat. "The exposure to the sun. But our world is one of power and deceit. You needed to see for yourself. I allowed it this time, knowing I could soon have Lenore ready to come to your rescue. Or you could have learned that another time, in a more life-threatening situation where no one would have been around to help you."

The words, a sharp reminder of what her future held, cut into her heart. She leaned against the wall and slid to the floor. Ethan joined her.

"The Strigoi," Ethan continued, "can track scents easily. Robert knew yours well because you two have met. He did not know the other scent was mine. If I'd been seen, too much would have been revealed. All of our efforts would have been for naught."

"Robert . . . followed my scent?" Ophelia asked. "All this way? But—"

"He appeared as your mother . . . something else he shouldn't be able to do. Clearly he has more ties than the average Strigoi. Maltorim ties."

She stared at the floor, trying to absorb all the implications.

Ethan lifted her chin, turning her face toward him. He swept away a dark lock of hair away from her cheek.

"If I don't do as I'm called, everyone will die. Including you . . . the woman I . . . the one . . . " He sighed and closed his eyes. "I don't deserve your forgi—"

She pressed her fingers to his lips, silencing him. A new depth reflected in his brown eyes, a darkness along the edges of his pupils. The golden flecks brightened them. "It's mine to give."

He kissed her then, his hand slipping along her jaw to cup her face.

"I'm glad you weren't harmed," he mumbled against her lips before closing his mouth over hers again.

Ethan's lips tasted of sugar and cloves, and Ophelia inhaled his heady aroma as she kissed him. Her stomach flopped and her mind clouded. In that moment, there was only Ethan, the gentle caress of his tongue, and the sense of all being *right* as she kissed him back, tentatively at first, and then with more abandon.

When he pulled back, Ophelia kept her eyes closed. She wasn't sure she could look at him.

"I love you, Ophelia. I should not, but I do. Though we can never be together, I cannot live out the rest of my eternity without you knowing that. I am sorry, truly, that I did not stop you from going after Robert."

God help her, she loved him, too, but their time together would soon end. She couldn't bring herself to say the words.

"Ye could have come after me," Ophelia said, though she knew that wasn't true.

"I needed to stay with Lenore while she finished her transformation. That opportunity might not have presented itself again. Perhaps . . . perhaps if I didn't think I could help Lenore quickly enough, I would have gone after you myself."

When Ophelia said nothing, he stepped away from her. "Being around you—this has challenged everything I believed I was confident in. If only you realized how easily you could break my resolve . . . ."

"I wouldn't," she replied quietly.

"I know," Ethan said. "That only makes this harder."

Ophelia couldn't take any more of the conversation. She excused herself to wash up and prepare dinner, and, after a quiet meal, she joined Ethan by the fire.

He sat in his chair; she, on the floor by his feet. She rested her head against his thigh to stare at the crackle of the fireplace flames. His fingers swirled along her scalp, and she closed her eyes, breathing in the cabin air that had filled with the warmth of charred wood despite the draft of the chill night breeze.

"How could Robert have looked just like my mother?"

"There is something happening within the Maltorim. As my guardian told me, it could be years—centuries perhaps—before anything comes of it. What that is, exactly, is part of your calling, not mine."

"The ritual with Lenore . . . Something went wrong, didn't it?"

"The ritual went as planned."

"And the raven?"

"There was no raven, Ophelia. There are Morts in the area. They won't come near you when you are with me, but they can still disillusion you. Further, Robert had you under his influence. That was the main source of your confusion, the main reason your actions defied your better senses. Now that you understand, it should not happen again."

Ophelia swallowed. "So now what?"

"Lenore will return. My worry is whether you are ready for what comes next. You need to be, and yet, we cannot change that you are not."

Kneeling up, Ophelia cupped her hands on the either side of Ethan's face. "I'm sorry I didn't trust you."

He grasped one of her wrists. "The problem is you don't trust yourself."

How could she? She'd been right about Robert, but how many things had she been wrong about? Hadn't she believed her mother's stories were only fairytales? Or was there some deeper part of her that had always known better? And yet, the night her father had died, she'd not sensed anything. Shouldn't she have felt something—known somehow that he was in danger?

Ethan stood and pulled Ophelia to her feet. With his hands resting on her hips, he took in a deep breath and closed his eyes for a long moment.

When he opened them, he dropped his hands away and walked over to sit on the cot. Ophelia waited, hoping for him to say something more, to make sense of the storm raging within her.

"My entire family was murdered," he said. He stared down at his hands. "I was too quick to trust the wrong person. To trust them instead of my own instincts."

Her heart thumped at the sentiment. She wanted to ask more, yet she could not bear to carry his heartache with her own. "Am I wrong to trust ye?"

"What would it mean for me to say no? If I am not worthy of trust, my answer is meaningless."

Ophelia padded closer. She touched his hair and smiled softly. "Not to me."

Ethan looked up. His hand found hers, and the warmth of

his fingers against her palm, his fingertips against her wrist, sent a tingling sensation through her entire body. He eased her closer until she stood between his knees, and with his other hand, he pulled her body down to his.

In the past, she would have stopped. She would not have allowed herself to have these feelings in the first place. She'd already lost everyone who ever meant anything to her, and she didn't need to set herself up for that kind of pain again. But Ethan's touch comforted her in this new, strange life.

"It is an insult to your worth for me to love you," he said, "but I cannot change the feelings you've ignited in me."

She leaned forward, toppling him back against the cot, and pressed her lips to his. He wrapped his arms around her and rolled her onto her back, tracing his kisses from her lips, down her jaw line, and to her collarbone.

As he shifted his weight up to kiss her again, his pelvis pressed closer to her own, and the heat between her thighs pulsed. He closed his lips over hers, and his tongue explored her mouth, touched her teeth, slid against her own tongue. His hand glided soothingly over the serpent's mark, and his fingers wrapped around the hair at the nape of her neck. Ophelia kissed him back heatedly, her hands moving along the strong planes of his back.

Ethan broke the kiss. He stared into her eyes, searching, tension forming in his jaw and a line creasing between his eyebrows. He pulled away and sat on the edge of the bed, and the mattress shifted, the wool blanket hushing as it rubbed against the sheets.

"I'm sorry," he said quietly.

Ophelia sat up and touched his shoulder. "Ye 'ave no reason to be."

He walked over to the fire, leaving Ophelia alone on the bed with an aching worry in her chest.

"Are ye all right?"

He chuckled sadly, shaking his head. "More than all right. But once you are inside the Maltorim, that will be our end."

Ophelia took a steadying breath and stared down at her hands. "Say I don't join the Maltorim?"

"That mark will kill you if you don't turn. And if you stay with me, we'll be hunted by other Guardians until you are captured and set right on your path. If I fail to see you to your calling, they will only move me to start fresh. Another girl, another place."

"So this is it? I can't 'ave a life of my own?"

"You are free to do as you wish, but I cannot be the reason you deny your calling. *I won't.*"

"I understand—"

"No, you don't."

"They can make their orders, but the decision would still belong to ye."

The corner of Ethan's lips turned up, as though to smile, but the expression was more of a grimace. "Everything isn't a choice. I accepted my calling long ago, and now I must go where they send me."

"Ye can't just say no?"

"It is for life. I have always gone willingly, but should they choose, they can move me where they need me, and there will be nothing I can do to stop it."

"That's not right. Ye should always have a choice."

"Sometimes we meet challenges. Other times we dodge consequences."

"We're being forced into this. There is nothing ye can say to change that."

"Then you plan to go through with your calling?"

Ophelia sighed, though it didn't release the weight on her chest; the confusion just kept crashing through her.

"What choice do I 'ave?" she asked wearily.

She wasn't sure where she stood anymore. What kind of 'choice' was this? Either she would sacrifice her own life to save humanity, or she would hold selfishly to the things she wanted in exchange for a life on the run. A life knowing her selfish choices had doomed herself and everyone else. Yes, her father had been right when he'd said she could never make up her mind . . . but this was more than that.

That night, as Ophelia closed her eyes and began to drift to sleep, she heard Ethan whisper, "I tried to go after you, Ophelia. I tried."

But she had not been meant to hear, and so she said nothing, kept her eyes closed, and pretended she was already asleep.

DAMASCUS, 1808

Shortly after nightfall, Lenore stumbled into the cabin, her boots clobbering across the dirt floor. She eased herself to the ground by the fireplace and rested on her back, wincing. Her hand clasped the amulet around her neck, and she closed her eyes. Ophelia almost choked on the smell—the rotting stink of burnt skin.

"Everything hurts," Lenore mumbled.

Ethan's gaze steadied on the open sores of Lenore's sun-blisters. "You spent the whole day outside?"

"It's been centuries."

Ethan strode over to the counter and prepared her a glass of his blood then brought it over to her.

"Elevate her head," he said to Ophelia. "She's too weak."

With a resolute nod, Ophelia kneeled on the ground beside Lenore. As she lifted the Cruor-girl's head into her lap, Lenore gasped, and Ethan hurried over with the glass of blood. He tilted the glass against her lips, but Lenore could barely swallow the blood. Her head lolled to one side, blood seeping out the corner of her mouth and dribbling down her chin and into the creases of her neck. The firelight danced over the spots of white on her teeth that were not coated in red.

Ophelia lifted her gaze to Ethan. "Will she be all right?"

"If we can get her to drink." To Lenore, he said, "Do you not think about these things? You should have returned hours ago."

"I haven't see the sun——" Lenore coughed. "——in two hund——"

For a second time, Ethan attempted to help Lenore drink the blood, and this time, she managed to swallow a few sips. Some color returned to her cheeks and her eyes brightened.

"Can you sit up?"

Lenore tried, but the effort seemed to take more of her energy, and Ethan told her to lay back and rest.

"She really needs human blood." He turned his deep brown, apologetic eyes to Ophelia. "Do you think . . . ?"

"Now?" Ophelia eyes went wide. "Ye want me to change *now?*"

Ethan nodded.

She took a shaky breath. Once she did this, there would be no turning back. Things would only get worse. She would be a monster, trapped to darkness, and she would be giving herself over to the dark deeds of the elemental council. How could she possibly reconcile that with the idea that any of this was for some greater good?

But just as Ethan had said, the mark of the serpent burned harsher with each passing hour, the Cruor blood becoming less effective as a topical ointment.

"I'm ready," Ophelia said finally, but the tightness in her throat betrayed her words.

Kneeling on the other side of Lenore, Ethan stared at Ophelia. The Cruor's breathing was stronger now, and her head steadied in Ophelia's lap.

"Ophelia," Ethan said gently, "I would have failed without you. You were strong in my moment of weakness. You are strong and fierce and beautiful. I can see now why you were chosen."

Ophelia swallowed and mumbled a quiet, "Thank you."

"Promise me—promise you will not mourn my loss when the time comes," Ethan said.

"What are ye saying?"

He clenched his jaw and shook his head. "If you're ready, we can begin."

"Ethan," she said sharply. "Tell me what you mean. What loss?"

"It's time," he said more fiercely this time.

Though her frustration boiled in her stomach and caused a tremble in her jaw, she let it go, and reached her forearm forward, in front of Lenore's mouth. Her arm was trembling, only to shake more furiously when Lenore's fangs snapped out.

Ethan nudged Ophelia's arm away.

"Wait," he said. "Not like that."

Ophelia lowered her arm to her side. Before she could question him, Ethan came around to sit behind her. She leaned back into his chest, and his lips brushed against her ear.

"I'm going to have to hold you, Ophelia. You are going to want it to stop while it's happening. Once this starts, there is no turning back. Are you certain you are ready?"

How could she be? An insistence born in her core, however, drove her actions now, and it was a force stronger than the serpent's burn. It was for her mother, her father, and the risks they took to protect her. It was for others like them who would suffer their fate.

"I'm ready," she said.

At first, Ethan's grasp on her wrist was gentle. A sadness swept over Lenore's face; perhaps it was fear, though Ophelia couldn't fathom what fear Lenore would have. Ophelia's heart pounded in her ears, the pressure filling her head and making the room spin.

Lenore's fangs pricked into Ophelia's flesh like twin thorns, at first only aching mildly. A haze seeped into Ophelia's mind, a shushing calm like a breeze bending the tall grass in the field. Her heart rate slowed, and her eyelids fluttered as a fatigue settled over her. Lenore's voice pulsed in her mind—a jumble of overlapping words . . . indistinct, meaningless . . . but Ophelia could feel them change her consciousness, burning a sense of *knowing* into her mind.

Lenore dug her fangs in deeper, the pressure uncomfortable and nauseating. Through the haze, Ophelia became aware of the blood gushing from her arm, soaking Lenore's face, neck, and clothes. The sloshing of Lenore feeding from her. No longer did Ophelia feel listless, as though she was floating atop a river; instead, she felt pinned between Lenore and Ethan, impaled by Lenore's bite and restrained by Ethan's ever-firmer grip on her wrist.

The icy bite mark itched, as though in the early stages of frostbite, and soon the chill branched out through the veins in her arms, so cold it burned. She needed to stay still, but soon the pain reached her shoulder, stronger with each passing moment, and she screamed. She tried to pull away, but Ethan's fingers dug deeper into her wrist and his other hand gripped her arm at the elbow. His biceps squeezed against her shoulders as he tried to keep her in place.

The jolt of trying to yank her arm away created a tear in her forearm, and Ophelia vomited at the sight of the wound, black and purple, her flesh unnaturally separated.

Lenore drank with her eyes closed, and, despite herself, Ophelia struggled to get out of Ethan's grasp. Pain shuddered through her entire body as the Cruor poison seeped into her blood and pumped a smoldering heat through her veins. Her heart thumped twice.

Then, it stopped.

DAMASCUS, 1808

WHEN OPHELIA AWOKE on the cot, the night was silent. Her throat ached with the persistent soreness of an early cold, though she wasn't at all feverish. An empty, eerie calm filled her chest. The room was quiet; she could not even hear the sound of her breath, and, for a moment, Ophelia thought she had lost her hearing. But then there was a rustling noise across the room.

Her gaze darted over to the fireplace, where Ethan still tended to Lenore.

Ophelia sat up. "Will she be all right?"

Her voice sounded strange, somehow lighter, and Ophelia touched her throat. His gaze locked on hers.

"The Cruor heal quickly."

"Am I . . . Well, I'm one of them now, aren't I?"

Ethan's jaw tensed, but he managed a quick, "Yes."

"My 'eart . . . " Ophelia started, but she couldn't bring herself to finish.

"It only *feels* like it's not beating," Ethan said. "It beats very slowly. Perhaps once per year, it is said."

"And I will not age."

"Millions of heartbeats will pass before you show the aging of a year."

"Millions of years?" Ophelia coughed, the ache in her throat worsening with each passing moment.

A low moan vibrated from Lenore's throat as she shifted to sit up. Her countenance improved before Ophelia's eyes. Lenore stretched and steadied herself, clutching the edge of the cot for a moment before she pushed herself to her feet. She stretched her neck from side to side and closed her eyes, seeming to hover between moments. When she opened her eyes, it was as though nothing had happened. All the wounds had healed.

"My heart beats more than that," she said. "At least once each day, at least once, with each remembrance of—" She clenched her jaw. "—of someone I lost."

The ache in Ophelia's esophagus intensified, turning into a burn far worse than the serpent's mark. Her tongue and the inside of her cheeks were so dry she feared they would crack and bleed. Hunger pains bloomed in her stomach. An image flashed through her mind—her teeth sinking into Ethan's neck. Draining him.

"Are you all right?" Ethan asked.

Lenore grinned. "You planned poorly, Ankou. Unless, you intended to be her first meal."

Ophelia shook her head. She clenched her hands to resist the urge to claw at her throat. "Stay away."

Ethan's brow furrowed, and he started to walk over, but Ophelia jumped to her feet and stepped back.

"I said stay away from me!"

Ethan halted, and the smile fell from Lenore's expression. The three stood frozen in that strange tableau while Ophelia's hunger grew more with each passing moment. With that pang, anger wound like a vine through her dead heart.

This was Robert's fault.

Without a word, Ophelia darted out the door and into the

field. In a blink of an eye, the cabin was far behind and she was already near the entrance of the grove where she'd seen her mother earlier. No, not her mother. *Robert.* She braced herself for the sudden halt, but her body was more agile now, and she came to a graceful stop. She glanced down at her body. How could such grace come from a monster?

The air carried Robert's scent—a husky soil-like aroma and the smell of charred wood. Ophelia could almost smell Lady Karina's house on his flesh, for all the time he spent there, often watching Ophelia's every move.

Now she knew what to make of the way he would leer at her as she mopped floors or prepared meals or helped Lady Karina freshen up for the day. It was lust, yes, but not for her, as she had assumed. No, Robert craved destruction and power.

She'd never forget the way he smelled, and now that her senses were stronger, she knew he was close. Robert had become an antelope in the field.

Ophelia whipped through woods, darting between branches, crunching over fallen saplings, ducking beneath low branches. She didn't stop until she reached his camp. He sat by a small fire, naked from the waist up, a large gash on his side seeping blood. White tissue protruded from the wound.

Robert didn't make a move, just sat there, staring unseeingly at the fire. "I knew you'd come for me."

"And yet ye remained 'ere."

"What use is running now? You've changed, and you'd have come for me eventually."

Ophelia shot over to where he sat, the fire casting her shadow over him. "Ye wanted me 'ere. Now I've come. Alone."

"You expect a fight?" he asked, gesturing to his wounds, wincing. "Do you think there is one for me to give?"

Robert's blood was meant to meet her need as well as

quench her thirst for revenge. But only if he was willing to fight.

Ophelia lifted her foot and kicked him in the shoulder, onto his back. Her fangs snapped down and she pounced on him. Her chest heaved with each heavy breath, the restraint not to sink her teeth into his throat becoming painful to her body.

"Fight," she commanded him.

Robert laughed. "I'd rather deny you the satisfaction."

Ophelia slammed her fist into the dirt beside his head and snarled. "I will kill ye either way."

"I am dead anyway," Robert said, "Failure has a price. Unless . . . " He steeled his gaze on Ophelia. "Allow me to bring you in. It would do us both a favor."

Ophelia's body shook from her restraint. "I care only to see ye die."

"Yet, you still have a mission, no? I know you weren't taken here for no reason. You were called, *weren't you?*"

She didn't need to answer. Branches crunched behind her, and Ethan's voice soon followed. "You underestimate the woman's scorn."

Ophelia glared at him. "Go away, Ethan. This doesn't concern ye."

Lenore stood at the edge of the clearing, arms crossed, looking on with smug amusement. Ophelia's gaze passed between them, then fell back to Robert. All she could see was the pulse in his neck. He was one of the Strigoi. He was one of the living, and his blood would sate her hunger.

"Ophelia," Ethan said softly. He walked up behind her. "You don't want to do this. Perhaps we should consider—"

"There is no we."

Ethan took out his blade and cut across his forearm.

"You'll feel better once you drink," he said. "You'll be able to think clearly. You won't feel so out of control."

"I am not out of control."

It was a lie, though one Ophelia wished were true. She could not stop shaking. The dry burn in her throat made her feel as though she was choking on her own blood. The blood flowing from Ethan's arm called to her—a primal need.

Please, don't let me be this monster.

The hunger took over, and Ophelia felt as though she were drifting outside herself. Her body thrust forward, her teeth sunk into the flesh of Ethan's arm. Blood, sweet and heavy, spurted into her mouth. It flowed down her esophagus, soothing the burn, easing the sores of cracked tissue.

She closed her eyes, floating away in her mind. Peace played over her nerves, arousing her senses. She could sense them all. Ethan grimaced. Lenore watched intently. Robert slunk into the shadows like the snake he was, but didn't leave as she wished he would.

Ethan's blood slowed.

Stop, now.

Her body shook, and she dug her nails into his arm to force herself to push away, but as she tried to open her mouth to release him, every part of her being resisted. A hand rested on her shoulder. Lenore's, she knew, as one would know the touch of their sire. And in that touch, Lenore's energy demanded that Ophelia stop, as did Ophelia's own will.

But her body still resisted.

Shaking, she forced her fangs to retract. Her eyes shot open. The moonlight stung her eyes, and she lifted her hand to shield them. The wet blood chilled on her teeth, lips, and chin, but Ethan only looked at her with concern.

She backed away. "I . . . I'm . . . "

"Shhh," Ethan said. "You'll learn your way. Within a few weeks, you'll rarely have to feed to keep that bloodlust at bay, and within several years you will be able to control your urges despite the difficulty."

The moments sobered Ophelia's thoughts. The haze had lifted, and now she was trapped in a body that had just acted in a way she could have never forgiven herself for only hours earlier.

"Lenore will hunt animal blood for you tonight," Ethan continued. "You and I—we'll have to talk with Robert."

The mention of Robert's name reignited the hatred bubbling in her gut, and her regrets and intended apologies died on her lips. She sneered at Robert, who had maintained his distance.

"Fine," she mumbled.

Fine, for now. But soon she would see to his death.

DAMASCUS, 1808

THEY TRAVELED BY NIGHT. Traveled by roads unseen, traveled with quiet steps and hushed whispers.

The world hummed in the background of Ophelia's thoughts. Once they arrived at the Maltorim's asylum, she would be expected to approach the entrance as though she were an uncivilized, newborn Cruor. Not that it was so far from the truth, but Lenore and Ethan said her bloodlust was minimal compared to most. The serpent's mark made sure of that, though at least the burning had stopped.

It wasn't as though Ophelia had never hidden truths about herself before, but this was different. This went beyond simple deceit and into the realm of false identities and fabricated stories. One misstep could mean her life. And Robert—she still resented his role in all of this. She needed his help, but she couldn't trust him.

Lenore, however, was not apprehensive. Ophelia knew because of their blood bond—because Lenore was Ophelia's sire. If Ophelia wanted the Maltorim to take her under their wing, she needed to convince them that her maker was dead. And Lenore was decidedly *very* alive.

If the Maltorim did not accept her, however, this would all have been for nothing.

As they strode on, Ophelia felt every emotion strumming through Lenore's body: the buzz, the excitement, the hunger—or was it thirst?—for adventure. Had Lenore not been so intrigued by their journey, Ophelia believed she would have taken leave by now. She could feel something more brewing there as well . . . some other driving-force that carried Lenore along with them on this journey . . . but a newborn cannot read the meaning behind all of their sire's emotions, and Lenore had certainly kept that corner of her heart well-guarded.

As they crested the next hill, the Maltorim's asylum expanded along the horizon. Stone walls encapsulated crowded rows of cemetery headstones and, in the center of the graveyard, a mausoleum—with its primeval doors and concrete edifice—awaited Ophelia's charade. She marveled at the crumbling limestone, having never before been able to see so clearly from such a great distance.

Ethan stopped, placing a hand on Ophelia's shoulder. The night's wind, carrying on it the scent of the dead and the grit of dirt, swept between her and Ethan, chilling the warmth of him at her back and lifting her hair from her neck.

"We'll stay until you're safely inside."

Ophelia swallowed. She didn't turn to face him, just stood there, studying the path they'd yet to travel. He hadn't stood this close to her since before they departed. She'd spent the journey half-wishing he would transport them through space, but he'd said they couldn't risk that. The Maltorim would be able to sense them if they did, whereas if they approached on foot, their supernatural presence would seem just a part of the usual world around them.

"It has to be this way," he said, but his voice died off in a whisper, and Ophelia was uncertain whether the sentiment was intended for himself or for her. "Remember one thing when faced with tribulations, Ophelia: Fight. Whatever you do, fight. That is the only way to survive in our world."

Lenore sighed the full weight of her irritation as Robert brushed past Ophelia and Ethan to start the road ahead. "Well, then," he said. "Come on if we're to do this."

Ophelia turned to Ethan and startled at the sudden proximity of his body. He hadn't felt so close standing at her back, but now here he was, his face inches above her own, his gaze pressing down into hers in a way that tightened her chest and shortened her breaths.

What she felt could not be imagined. Surely the desire burned as deeply in him as it did in her. Surely the heat spread through his body with the same intensity and need. It was there, between them. Of that Ophelia was certain. And yet she could see in his regretful brown-gold eyes the same understanding that resided in her heart.

"Perhaps—" she started, but he stepped away, his expression turning stony and his gaze averting to the distance. A cold breeze rushed by, moving Ethan's dark hair, and his eyes watered. The pale moon washed out his bronzed skin, and the stubble on his jaw looked darker by contrast.

"Good luck, Ophelia." He didn't look at her.

"Of course," she said quietly, folding her hands in front of her. "To ye as well, Sir Ethan Forrester of Rome."

She turned away, hoping to hide the tears that moistened her eyelashes. She clenched her fist, the dig of her fingernails in her palm a welcome distraction from the heartache pulsing in her chest. In her mind, she turned back around and demanded more from him. She yelled at him and cried to him. But even in her thoughts, that did no good. Ethan had accepted what needed to be done. And so Ophelia continued her quiet march away, farther and farther from him, hoping for the very thing she felt hopeless of, as though maybe if she stood there long enough, reality could be erased and the moment could be reenacted in a new way.

Finally she found her own inner resolution and took the first few steps away—the hardest steps—and from behind her she heard Ethan curse beneath his breath. She nearly crumbled, so evident and raw was his pain, but she only hesitated, her next step shakier than the last. She couldn't turn around now or she would fall apart, so she bit her lip and leaned into her next few steps, starting down the road to close the distance between her and Robert.

After she'd gone a few yards, Lenore called out, "I want to know everything. You'll know where to find me."

There was a bumping sound—perhaps Ethan nudging Lenore—and some sharp, quiet words that Ophelia could not discern. She didn't respond. That Lenore could keep in contact with Ethan stirred within Ophelia a fiery anger.

Just outside the cemetery, Robert stopped short and pivoted toward her. "You'll have to bite me now, if they're to understand why I'm bringing you in."

Her stomach bubbled with a mix of hunger and disgust, but when Robert loosened his collar and stretched his neck, Ophelia's fangs snapped down. She closed her eyes, trying to listen to the howl of the wind between the graves to block out the sound of her mouth on his flesh—to block out her teeth piercing his flesh—but it was all for naught. The sound reverberated in her ears and echoed in her mind with a sickening crunch, but as the blood sloshed into her mouth, pulsing between her lips, the thrum of the life-blood overrode her inhibitions.

It was loud and insistent—a carnal thrumming. The blood flowed sweet, like gooseberries and cherry blossoms

Robert grabbed her hair and yanked back. "That's enough."

The blood coated her tongue and teeth and soaked her lips, chin, and cheeks. She'd been completely unaware of him as she'd fed, but now she could see the tension in his jaw, the pain evident by the creases around his eyes.

"My body will reject your poison," he said. "Don't worry."

She wasn't worried.

She stepped back, remembering just who this man was. He might be her way to get into the Maltorim's asylum—to gain their trust—but he was still the man who'd played a role in her parents' end.

"Let's carry on, shall we?" he asked flatly, though it didn't sound much like a question.

As much as Ophelia didn't want to speak with him more than necessary, she had to know. She needed to gather as much about this world as she could. "Is it true of all Strigoi, then? Can ye all expel the poison of the Cruor?"

"Nothing is ever that simple, Ophelia. We are each what we are, and we are each unique."

"Even me?"

"I've agreed to get you into the Maltorim only because of Ethan's promise to me. Once I've done my part, I owe you nothing."

She stopped and turned sharply toward him. "What promise?"

He shoved her shoulder and pointed ahead. "The entrance is that way. Through the mausoleum doors, behind a loose board, and straight ahead to the first door. Go through and you will find a man. You'll be safe with him until I arrive, though I suggest you say as little as possible."

She stared him down, but he was unrelenting. Whatever agreement Ethan and Robert had come to, she might never know. After releasing Robert from her scowl, Ophelia gave a slow nod and turned to pick her way toward the cemetery gate. Once through, she increased her pace until she was erratically jolting between headstones, through the entrance and up to the door Robert had directed her to approach.

The movement lingered behind her in a blur, and, as she stood staring at the large oak door, she felt something pulling her back. At first, she thought it was the after-effect of coming to a stop after such swift movement, but after a few more moments passed, she realized the pull remained, and it came from just a foot behind her.

She turned around and studied the ground. Light from the candle sconces glinted off a piece of brass peaking up from beneath the dirt.

Ophelia knelt down and brushed at the dirt—the same claylike dirt that packed the wooden-beam-supported walls. A knocker-like handle jutted out, attached to a small door in the ground.

The large door behind her creaked open, and she spun around, her eyes wide and taking in the man that now filled the doorframe. His expression was soft, his skin dark, his eyes darker. The crease between his eyebrows likely came from studying her condition: her torn, soiled dress; her disheveled hair; her blood-stained face. She remained frozen, crouched by the ground, but kept her head turned toward him despite the painful tension the odd angle created in her neck.

His brow furrowed, and Ophelia stared at him with wide eyes.

"Bist du in Ordung?" He studied her and shook his head. "Jól vagy? Er alt i orden?"

He started to step forward, but then seemed to think the better of it. Finally, he shook his head and squatted beside her, putting his hand between her shoulder blades. "Är du okej?"

Realization dawned on Ophelia. He was trying to ask her something, but didn't know where she was from. "My maker is dead."

As the man nodded, his coarse hair, tightly woven into strands, brushed his shoulders. "You've come to the right place. I'm Adrian. And you?"

"Ophelia."

At that moment, Robert burst through the door. He feigned being out of breath, hunched over and sucking in gulps of air. Ophelia had to turn her head to hide her amusement.

"She," he said, panting, "tried to"—he sucked in another breath—"kill me."

Adrian's gaze passed from Robert back to her. "*This* woman?"

Robert plugged his hands onto his hips and straightened, tossing his chin up. "She's stronger than she looks."

Adrian narrowed his eyes. "Pity she wasn't a little stronger."

"Well? You're going to take her to the Queen then, yes?"

Adrian's gaze swept skeptically over Robert. "Do you have any grievances?"

"No. But I prefer to tell the Queen myself. The girl could perhaps be of use. For certain, she needs help, but I did see some restraint."

"So you chased down your attacker. How unusual." Adrian's gaze shifted to Ophelia, then back to Robert. "Excuse me, please, but I'm inclined to ask what your investment is in this girl. It's not often a shifter would release a newborn from consequence in a situation such as this."

"I'd hate to see a final end to such a beautiful specimen, is all," Robert said.

Grinning, Robert shifted his gaze to Ophelia, and he made no effort to hide the way his attention slipped down to her breasts. It took every bit of restraint Ophelia had not to lash out, but as much as she hated him, she knew she needed him. Worse, she had to pretend to be grateful for his intervention. She lowered her gaze to her hands, now clasped in front of her waist, and mouthed a silent 'thank you'.

Adrian pressed his lips together and nodded. "Right. Of course. This way, then."

He removed one of the torches mounted on the wall and started down the long passage. Robert tilted his head after him, but Ophelia stood firm, motioning with her gaze for

Robert to go ahead. He might be helping her, but this man was still not to be trusted.

Robert's grin widened.

"As you wish," he whispered, starting ahead of her.

Oh, he was sickening in the way he found pleasure in her fear of him, but now was not the time to let her emotions get in the way. She followed, each step causing the emptiness where her heart should beat to grow. For all she knew, he would turn her over for being the child of a dual-breed the moment they came into the Queen's company.

The hall twisted at odd angles, a strange labyrinth that slanted forever downward, deeper into the earth, the air growing colder, moister, until they reached new halls made of stone so damp and cold that Ophelia felt as though she'd traveled through fields of rain. The halls, with their high ceilings and stony floors, harbored the stink of mold, and the farther they descended, the more the blocks decayed and the mortar between them eroded.

She could see through the darkness as though it were daylight, and she wondered what purpose the torch Adrian grasped could truly serve. Studying him, she took in the tense muscles of his neck and shoulder, took in how tightly his hand wrapped around the handle of the torch.

A weapon.

She smirked at the back of Robert's dimwitted skull. Adrian didn't trust him, either.

Robert cracked his neck, then craned his head toward their guide. "You know, Adrian . . . "

Adrian spun around, the flames flickering inches from Robert's face and casting a yellow glow over both their expressions. Robert flinched, but his smile did not waver.

"Know what?" Adrian asked.

"I was just going to say. Your parents and mine—"

Adrian turned around again and strode farther down the hall. "My parents are dead."

No one said anything for the rest of the descent to the Queen's room, the strain in the air between the men palpable. They knew each other. Of course they did—Robert had been here before. Robert, so he said, was a favorite of the Queen's. In his version of every story, Queen Callista was a woman who loved anyone willing to betray their own kind for her benefit.

Once they reached a door encrusted with jewels, Adrian requested Robert and Ophelia wait a moment while he alerted the Queen of their arrival. As they stood outside, Ophelia's mind wandered. How long would Ethan and Lenore stay nearby? Perhaps Ophelia could reunite with them once things settled.

She was too nervous about meeting with Callista to think of anything relevant—what she would say to the Queen, for instance. If this Queen suspected for a second that Ophelia was lying, she would surely kill her.

In that moment, Ophelia wanted to turn and run. To run so hard and fast that time would erase itself. All the way back to Lady Karina's estate, where she would decline delivering the letter and accept punishment for her disobedience. Ophelia sucked in a deep breath. Her inability to change things left her restless, and she tried to will her body to stop trembling, but it was no use.

She'd never had a choice. The serpent's mark, which she was still burdened with keeping hidden, had enslaved her. She lifted her hand and touched her neck. No more burning. No more pain. But what sort of life did she have now? What kind of 'life' could any Cruor live?

Part of her blamed Ethan. But as soon as she tried to harness that grudge—to focus on it and use it to guide her—the emotion softened. She could still see the hard lines of his face. His eyes were just as sharp but belied a deeper pain. For all his strength, he was a wounded man. A man in hiding. Soon, she would be in hiding, too.

She could go to him eventually. Couldn't she?

The door creaked open and Adrian stepped out. "The Queen will see you now."

The Queen, standing eerily close to Adrian's back and at least a whole foot shorter than him, smiled thinly to her guests. Her velvety black dress clung to her chest and stomach, and the hem swished to the floor and pooled at her feet, her bare toes peeking out. She was unnaturally thin, unnaturally pale, and unnaturally pleasant-looking. Almost-white hair fell past her shoulders, and she wiped a spot of blood from the corner of her mouth and extended her delicate hand.

"Hello, Robert," she said.

Beyond her—beyond this girl who looked more child than woman—awaited a dark room with a long table sheltered by a white tablecloth and flickering candlelight.

In the middle of the room, a lifeless body sprawled across the gold-leafed granite floors.

DAMASCUS, 1808

As Queen Callista stepped aside and swept her arm toward the room, two young men came forward and cleared away the dead woman.

Callista's brow furrowed. "Is everything all right?"

It was the first time Callista acknowledged Ophelia's existence.

Ophelia nodded firmly and took several timid steps into the large room. The ceiling seemed to stretch impossibly high, so high that it became lost in the darkness. Was there any ceiling at all, or did the room just stretch up to the dark night?

Just then, a chandelier lit up overhead. The room became suddenly smaller, and Ophelia felt trapped. A hand, cold and unnerving, touched Ophelia's arm. She spun around with a gasp.

"Jumpy, are we?" Queen Callista asked, one side of her mouth twisting into a smirk. "Please, sit. Adrian has explained a bit, though I must admit to having many questions to ask you myself."

Somewhere behind Ophelia, Robert moved. She could feel it was him—shuffling forward, joining them inside the room. His grin beamed into the back of her head.

Queen Callista's smile tightened.

"It's not very polite," she said through her teeth, "to remain standing when your Queen has invited you to sit."

With that, the Queen, smoothing her gown beneath her, took a seat at the head of the table. There were two chairs awaiting Ophelia and Robert on one long side. On the other side, four young men—boys, really—sat in a stoic row, their gazes unwavering, their eyes as coal-black as their hair, and their skin as pale as moonlight.

Ophelia could not bring herself to move as swiftly as the Queen surely expected, but she took the seat furthest from the Queen and stared at the boy directly across from her. Anything would make a better focal point than the Queen.

Robert sat beside her. The door to the room clicked shut, and Robert immediately jumped back up again.

"My Queen, this woman"—he pointed at Ophelia—"has come here to—"

Ophelia shot to her feet and lunged at Robert, fangs already snapped down. She had him pinned to the ground, her hair spilling forward to hide her view of the rest of the room.

Robert pushed at her chest, holding her at a distance. "She has come to infiltrate the Maltorim."

"Liar!" Panic rushed into Ophelia's lungs, but the anger over Robert's betrayal was stronger. And also no surprise at all. "Robert is the one who intends harm."

The room stilled. Queen Callista rose from her chair, her fingertips pressing down against the tabletop. She arched one thin eyebrow and stared down at Ophelia. "Can you prove the truth of what you say?"

Ophelia managed a nod but could not bring herself to words. There was only one option left—one thing Ethan had told her to do if things went sour, and one thing that Ophelia most did not want to do.

"There are others," she said finally. "Robert brought me to

distract ye while they close in. Otherwise why waste this time on me, when 'e could 'ave ensured my death the moment I arrived?"

In one swift movement, Callista removed a sword from over the door and sliced through Robert's neck. His head rolled across the room. Ophelia stood and stepped away, the back of her wrist to her mouth as her stomach surged.

The Queen tilted her head, grinning.

"Well, we wouldn't want to have any traitors in our midst, would we?" The grin broadened. "I never much liked him anyway."

Ophelia was too stunned to move. She couldn't avert her gaze from Robert's decapitated body, from the blood spilling onto the marble floor. This had been what she wanted, hadn't it? He'd played a role in the murders of her parents. He'd tried to betray her, to have her killed. But with Callista standing there, the sword hanging lazily from her hand, Ophelia felt more terrified now that he was dead.

Callista returned the sword to its mantle then turned back to the room. Behind her, the tip of the blade dripped blood to the floor. She was still smiling. "We'll track the others. I'm sure Ophelia won't mind pointing us in the right direction. After all, she's so concerned for our well-being. Isn't that right, Ophelia?"

There was nowhere to go from here but forward. "Of course, my Queen."

Ophelia, however, had no intentions of guiding the Queen to her friends.

CALLISTA DID NOT TRAVEL LIGHT. She brought with her four men. They walked two ahead of the Queen and two behind, and the Queen kept Ophelia close to her side, holding her hand as though they were long friends. Ophelia couldn't remember the way she'd come, but she did her best to guide them in false directions. There would be a dead animal around here somewhere . . . left behind by Lenore to throw the Maltorim off their tracks.

There it was. Just ahead.

The men in front halted and turned so abruptly that the words died on Ophelia's tongue. The taller of the two men dipped his head to the Queen. "We've picked up on her scent. Two or three hours prior. Perhaps we should follow."

Ophelia shook her head. "I'm certain they're right up ahead."

Callista closed her eyes and swayed her head. "Don't concern yourself with remembering the way, my dear. My men are the very best, I promise you. We will find these traitors yet."

And together they set off in the right direction, Ophelia struggling to shuffle forward as though her shoes were filled with hardened clay.

There were only so many promises Ophelia could make to herself then. Promises that Lenore and Ethan would be long gone by now, that she had distracted the search party long enough. Promises that they would have covered their tracks. But none of that meant anything to the Maltorim. With each new path traversed, Ophelia could feel the distance between herself and Lenore growing shorter. Soon she could smell Ethan on the air, and certainly she would not be the only one.

The closer they drew, the more Ophelia panicked. Her mind spun too quickly to formulate a plan—too quickly for any idea to form. Her chest tightened, and her voice constricted in her throat. What could she say to divert the Maltorim's efforts? One false move would result in her death.

So it was with regret that her gaze met Ethan's in the small field just north of the cemetery. He was standing with Lenore just several feet behind him, as though he were waiting, expecting this. Neither made any effort to escape or conceal themselves.

Lenore crossed her arms and slung her narrow gaze at Ophelia. "I should have known."

"Lenore, I didn't—"

Queen Callista laughed, the sound musical and at the same time tinny. "Oh, you're quite all right, Ophelia. We'll take care of them."

That was the furthest thing from what Ophelia wanted. And what if they realized Lenore was her maker?

Lenore clicked her tongue and stepped up beside Ethan. "If she would betray us," she said to the Queen, "what makes you think she won't betray you?"

"Betray me?" The Queen giggled, but then her expression turned cold and her fangs snapped down. "It really is not worth betraying me. Just ask your friend, Robert."

When Lenore didn't respond, the Queen smirked, one side of her mouth curving up and her gaze shifting playfully to the side. "Oh, that's right. Robert's hardly in the position to answer any questions. I'm afraid he won't be able to join you . . . ever again."

Ophelia stepped forward to claim she hadn't betrayed anyone, but Ethan's warning gaze settled over her body and an understanding swept in. Lenore didn't really think Ophelia betrayed them. Lenore would know that for a fact—Lenore would have felt all of this coming, such was the strength of a bond between maker and child. This had always been their alternate plan.

Callista and her men encircled Lenore and Ethan, but Ophelia stood back. She could not fight against them any more than she could fight with them. Before the Queen's men could take another step, Lenore and Ethan had two of them disabled, pinned to the ground, stakes driven through their hearts. The soldiers decomposed, their essence crumbling in the light breeze and scattering between patches of dead grass.

As the remaining men lunged for Ethan and Lenore, Ophelia had the sudden urge to run. But she could not. There was nothing she could do now but stand there hopeless, praying to a God she no longer believed existed.

Lenore struck with amazing speed. The man attacking her stumbled back but did not lose his ground. Locking arms, each struggled for the upper hand, their weight shifting back and forth until finally Lenore tackled him to the ground. Meanwhile, Ethan did not fare so well. Ankou were not a strong match against the Cruor.

Callista sidled closer to Ophelia and whispered, "Does it not make for a show?"

Ophelia smiled uneasily. She could barely force herself to nod. She winced as the blow one of the men delivered to Ethan echoed with a resounding crack. His eye swelled and blood gushed from his mouth, and the man attacking him was prepared to finish with the kill.

Ophelia trembled, and her stomach clenched. *Please, Lord, no. Not Ethan.* To her left, Callista was nearly bouncing on her toes, her eyes wide and glazed in delight. She and Lady Karina would have made fast friends.

A silence fell beside them. The head of one of the men flew past Callista, draining the color from her face and drawing out a gasp. Lenore had killed her attacker.

Callista stumbled back as Lenore advanced. Her eyes had gone dark—not black, but surely dimmed, faded, as though cast in shadows. Callista trembled and turned her pouting yet demanding face toward Ophelia. The look—being that of a helpless child—threw Ophelia off her senses.

"Do something!" the Queen demanded. She called past Ophelia to the man, her voice wavering. "Get the girl! Get the girl!"

The man immediately complied, pouncing on Lenore before she could reach the Queen.

Before Lenore turned to fight, Ophelia could hear her maker's voice in her mind: *You must honor the Queen.*

Through the cottony feeling in Ophelia's ears, she could hear what Callista had been shouting all this time.

"You! Ophelia, the man!"

Ophelia swiveled her head toward her.

Callista was pointing at Ethan. "Him! Kill him at once!"

Me?

Ethan paused, his gaze pleading. But pleading for what?

For you to honor the queen! came Lenore's sharp thoughts, cutting into Ophelia's own.

I can't.

You must.

But Ophelia could only stand there, her gaze shifting from the Queen to Ethan and Lenore's battle with one of the Queen's men.

Ethan shook his head before pouncing forward, knocking Ophelia to the ground. A short wind rushed from Ophelia's lungs, and a sharp ache shot up her spine.

"Ethan," she whispered.

He pressed his body against hers, pinning her down fiercely. His face lowered beside her own.

"We must fight," he whispered back, his voice low in her ear. "And you must win."

Though she struggled to free herself, she knew not what she would do once she had. But Ethan rolled to his back, pulling her on top of him in a way that gave the illusion she'd garnered the upper hand.

"Kill him!" the Queen screamed.

Ophelia's fangs snapped down in response to Ethan's bleeding wounds and to her arousal at his body pressed so close to hers. So tormented was she, trying to fight off her carnal nature, that she could not think of what to do.

Ethan's mouthed the words to her: *Kill me.*

The scent of his blood ignited her hunger, but her love for him was stronger than her bloodlust. Her heart begged the

Universe that her love for him could overcome this battle as well.

Tears sprung to her eyes, and she pounded her fist against his chest. *How can you ask this of me? How can you?*

"It's me or it's both of us," he whispered. "You must."

Even to Ophelia's newly heightened senses, the words were nearly inaudible, and the cries of war between Lenore and the remaining Queen's soldier nearly drowned out his voice. This only made the words more vulnerable, made them sharper in Ophelia's chest.

But hadn't this been the very reason she'd fallen for Ethan? That he'd been so devoted to this cause, so willing to sacrifice? She hadn't expected *this*, though. Deep down, from her very core, she'd hoped whatever bloomed between them that was stronger than any battle they would face.

Ethan's gaze travelled the length of her thigh, and then down to her calf. Her dress had ripped, revealing the stake tied with old cloth to her left boot. She looked at it and back to him, her head shaking with too little inclination for anyone but him to know her meaning.

No.

She could not kill him. No, no matter how many lives depended on it, this was simply asking too much. The Universe could find someone else. Find someone else to send into the Maltorim to do their bidding, for it would not be her. Ophelia would be killed by the Queen herself. The Universe could find someone else to do their bidding.

Ethan snatched the stake from Ophelia's boot and pressed it to her chest, forcing her hands to hold the jagged piece of wood as well. She could feel it splintering in her palms as she pressed back.

"Please, Ethan," she whispered, tears splashing off her nose and onto his cheeks. Another salty tear slid onto her lips. "I can't."

Though his arms shook with the façade of struggle, he

lowered the stake closer to his own heart. No matter how it might seem to the Queen, this was not a battle Ophelia could ever win. Ethan was far stronger.

"What are you waiting for?" the Queen bellowed.

Lenore, covered in blood and leaving a dead body in her wake, plummeted toward the Queen and knocked her to the ground. Her thoughts rushed out to Ophelia: *Save her and run.*

This was her chance. She shook her head at Ethan, releasing the stake and darting toward the Queen. She pushed Lenore from the Queen's body, using the force of the pent up anger she'd stored throughout her 'battle' with Ethan. Lenore tumbled backward, and Ophelia yanked the Queen to her feet and tugged her by the hand, running off. Lenore and Ethan chased them with some restraint for a short distance, then fell back and eventually disappeared into the horizon.

When they reached the mausoleum, Ophelia released the Queen and spun toward her.

The Queen slapped Ophelia on the cheek.

Ophelia was too stunned to speak. She raised her hand to her cheek, the slap having stung but without delivering any real pain.

"Good for nothing!" Eyebrows pinched together and a scowl on her face, Callista looked toward the golden glow on the horizon.

"We must get inside. Come next nightfall, your training will begin. If you cannot be trained, you'll be disposed of." She leaned in close to Ophelia. "I don't know what you expected, coming here, but you'd better make yourself useful."

Rumors of Ophelia spread throughout the Maltorim. Though it was still believed she had twice saved the Queen's life, some would say she had also twice brought the Queen's life to danger. It would be a long time before anyone would trust Ophelia, and not long after that, Ophelia would chance her position on the Maltorim to betray them again.

FROM DAMASCUS TO AL HARAH, 1809

OVER THE MONTHS, the Maltorim's attention on Ophelia wavered. She was no longer new or interesting. Even her bloodlust had died away, leaving her only the need to hunt once a fortnight. She'd come full circle—the equivalent of a scullery maid to the Maltorim, easily overlooked as though she were merely a part of the mausoleum's structure. A wall sconce, perhaps.

Here, in this mausoleum, she would lie in wait for some unknown girl, some girl Ophelia would somehow recognize when the time came. However long it would take—years, centuries—Ophelia would have to wait, a clandestine mole.

Tonight, the Maltorim was busy preparing for the Queen's five thousandth year. She was the oldest known vampire, having lived in the settlement of the Barada basin. She'd been buried alive at the age of fifteen and had taken nearly five thousand years to be reborn by the earth.

It was then she'd risen, sometime around 4800BC, her flesh and blood regenerated by the Universe, to travel far and wide to find others like her. It wasn't until nearly a century later that she found another of her kind in Anatolia. She declared the man her servant, and together they continued their travels, each century bringing forth more of the Cruor species.

But Ophelia knew Callista's story was a lie. Several months prior, while most of the Maltorim was tucked away in one of the chambers for an evening meeting, Ophelia was asked to tidy the Queen's room.

"Just make the bed and mop the floors," the Queen said. "*Don't* touch anything."

No one would dare touch the Queen's belongings. Except, perhaps, a woman such as Ophelia who had nothing to lose anymore.

Once the Queen departed, Ophelia peered out the door and down the halls and, seeing no one, eased the door so that it was only slightly ajar. Wide open would give her no warning, and closed entirely would draw attention. Everyone had something to hide, and if Ophelia was to survive here, she needed to know what truths had been hidden about the Queen.

The cleaning would wait. Being caught without the cleaning done would carry a lesser fate than being caught rummaging through Queen Callista's belongings, so Ophelia needed to get the latter out of the way.

She checked the usual places first. Under the pillow, under the mattress, inside the wardrobe. Nothing. There were no floorboards to check beneath. Ophelia plugged her fists onto her hips and scanned the room. It was mostly bare. All that remained was a bookshelf and a chair.

Where would Ophelia hide something if she were the Queen? Callista was too smart to make an obvious choice. Ophelia sighed and sat in the chair. It would take too long to go through the Queen's bookshelf. She gripped the sides of the parlor chair and squeezed her eyes shut.

Think.

She hunched forward and rested her head in her hands.

Something rustled beneath her, and Ophelia was struck with an idea.

She glanced to the door and, sensing no movement on the other side, slid to the floor and peeked at the underside of the chair. There it was. A leather-bound, beaten journal strapped to the bottom of the seat.

Ophelia slid the journal from its place, her heart thundering in her chest. The book felt soft and vulnerable in her grasp. She forced herself to drop her gaze from the doorway to the journal. She would need to know the moment someone walked by, but she couldn't read the journal and keep watch at the same time.

She had a lifetime to read, yes? Maybe just a few passages here and there . . . maybe that would be all it took. Some stolen moments like these. The risk of being caught was great, but the risk of not learning the truth . . . that could be greater.

That was the first night she cracked open the journal, careful not to disturb the pages, and began to read.

Over the months, Ophelia learned enough to empower her against the Queen should the need ever arise. She learned the truth about Callista—learned that her story was one told to gain followers, nothing more.

The story the Queen told belonged not to her, but to her father. A father who had abandoned her after killing her mother, following the discovery that Callista's mother was dual-natural—Strigoi and Cruor both—and that his daughter was dual-natured as a result. After Callista's father disowned her, she murdered him, though she kept alive his hatred for the dual breeds. A hatred for herself.

It was then she'd set out to find other Cruor.

Callista's chance for redemption had come in the form of a dream—one that led her not only to more of her kind, but also to other species she was destined to join to form a council for the Universe. Because of her stories, all of the elemental races believed the Maltorim had been called on by the

Universe, but the truth was that the Universe had never formed the Maltorim.

Callista had but one hope—the magic of the Ankou. But their magic came with risks Callista could not bring herself to face, nor could she risk word getting out that she was dual-natured. Some might not care; she was the Queen, after all. Others might see her being dual-natured as a reason to overthrow her reign.

Ophelia shook her head every time she thought of it; though Callista's father hated the dual breeds, Callista herself had nursed hatred into genocide, meanwhile allowing her followers to believe she was the purest of all Cruor—a true earthborn, and the first of their kind.

Ophelia dared not breathe a word of her knowledge to anyone, for her thoughts were the same as the Queen. True, they might overthrow her reign if they learned the truth, but alternately they might stand beside her despite her nature, which could very well mean Ophelia's own death, should she have been the one to announce her findings.

Ophelia would save her knowledge as a last resort.

Tonight, the rest of the Maltorim would celebrate the Queen. She was to be presented with a true Damascus sword, the steel blade laddered and waved with roses. This would be Ophelia's chance to slip away from the mausoleum, if only for a time. Her chance to put her calling aside and follow the pull of her heart.

A chance she was not supposed to take but refused to deny.

Ophelia stepped into the brisk night, leaving behind the loud chatter of the crowds, the music, and the spicily scented air of Queen Callista's celebration. Ophelia sped toward the distance without any direction in mind. Only away. When she was certain the distance she'd travelled was far enough—certain all of the Maltorim were too involved in their celebrations to notice her missing—she closed her eyes and felt with all her soul which way she needed to head next.

She walked with purpose. She traveled the length of several cities, crossed through many small towns, thankful her uncanny speed as a Cruor allowed her to travel so far in mere moments.

Ethan was out here, somewhere beneath this same dark moon. Lenore's presence she could always feel, a steady undercurrent in her body at all times, but her connection to Ethan was something tender, something hidden in a quiet corner of her soul.

She plowed through forests and over uprooted trees, stopping only when she reached a wood that a forest fire had recently claimed. What a shame the rain brewing in the air hadn't come sooner, come before the dry earth and bright sun had set fire to this beautiful land. By her feet, a daffodil struggled to survive, and a lone butterfly sought life in the young flower. How she wished Ethan was with her, wished he was there to restore the forest to its greatness.

She would find him yet.

Perhaps she was mad. Perhaps what she felt—the pull that led her—was not really there at all. But the energy in the air guided her through shadowed woods, across vulnerable fields and into the crumbling walls of the outer city limits, until she reached a large building made of many small rooms. One of the windows was blocked by a thick blanket. Ophelia strode over and stood beneath it.

"Ethan," she whispered loudly.

No response.

What was she thinking?

She shook her doubts away and lifted a small stone from the ground and tossed it at the window.

"Ethan," she hissed again.

Again, no response.

"Aye, I've right lost my mind," she mumbled to herself.

That twist in her gut—it'd been more heartache than instinct. And for what? Even if she had found him, he would have only sent her away. He would never allow her to risk everything.

She rubbed her hand against her cheek and bit her lip, closing her eyes. Why did her heart have to betray her this way? Why could she not hate Ethan instead? Why not despise him for being the one to usher her into this world?

"Ethan," she said to empty room above. "I'm sorry. I am sorry, though ye will never know that I came here tonight. I'm sorry that my heart got in the way. Sorry for loving ye."

She choked on those last words, then sucked in a resolved breath. This was no good. She needed to move on. But she could not get her feet to move nor her gaze to leave the window. Could not get her gaze to leave that square of hope. So badly she wanted him that she could smell his sweet clove scent on the night air.

"Ophelia?"

The voice came from behind her, arresting the space in her chest where her heart would have normally sped.

It was him.

She held her breath and spun around. Moonlight lit the sky behind him. He stood unmoving, his gaze covering every inch of her, her emotions swaying slowly from disbelief to desire.

"Ophelia," he said, with more confidence.

He strode over to her, and she threw her arms around him and kissed him deeply. He pressed her back against the wall in the alley, his hands sliding around her waist. He stopped, tilting his forehead against hers, his eyelashes tickling her brow.

"You've come to me," he said. He kissed her again, as though unable to keep his lips from her mouth. Finally he broke away and pulled her a few steps further down the alley to a wooden door and then inside.

Neither of them said a word until after he'd led her down the hall, up the stairs, and into a small, bare room that contained little more than cot, end table, and washbasin. He locked the door and turned to her again, shaking his head. "You shouldn't have come."

She stepped up to him, closing the distance between them, and kissed him with the passion she'd been holding back for far too long. She did not know when she would see him again, but she knew she would not give him up, knew she would not sacrifice him.

He put his hands to her shoulders, as if to stop her, but then held her tight and deepened the kiss, backing her up until her calves hit the foot of the bed. She cupped her hands around his face, breaking the kiss. His skin was paler than usual, his hair unkempt and the circles beneath his eyes dark.

"Ye are not well," she said.

"I will be fine, my love. I will be fine."

"What of the work ye are supposed to do?"

He shook his head slowly. "It is done. There was no calling for me beyond your delivery to the Maltorim. That is it for me."

"Oh, Ethan," she breathed, frowning. "'ow could ye say such a thing?"

"I have failed even that, if you are here now. What happened?"

He had not failed. No matter what anyone said, they deserved the hope they found in each other's company. "I am with them still! I am sure I can hold my place with them for many years."

He pulled back. "You need to return immediately. You cannot stay here."

"We are together," Ophelia said fiercely. "Don't tell me that is wrong."

He stared at her a long moment, unspeaking, and she feared her chest might cave beneath the silence. "You should go. I shouldn't have allowed this, shouldn't have entertained these ideas."

As he stepped away, Ophelia reached out and grasped his hand to tug him back. "Don't ye dare say that."

He was too close to her now to look at her as a package to be delivered. He could only look into her eyes. He could only face down her soul. Let him try to back away to that, let him try to back away from his own heart.

"Would ye still be standing here if this was not meant to be? Would not the Universe 'ave taken ye from me?"

For a long moment, Ethan stared at her, his pained expression softening. Ophelia knew she was right, and surely he knew as well. The Universe would grant them this one gift in their otherwise dire existence. They would have each other.

Ethan lifted her onto the bed, climbing between her knees as he lay her back and pressed his mouth to hers. His hands, shaky and uncertain, fumbled to undo her dress. He swept her hair away from her neck, leaving it to fan out its inky blackness on his sheets.

He removed her gown, kissed her ribs, grazed his lips over her breasts. As he placed kisses along her jaw and neck, she tilted her head back.

Then, they were falling. Falling through time and space. But this was different from when Ethan had moved her this way before. This time they moved through space as though floating through water toward the bottom of a lake.

She kissed the space behind his ear, traced her lips against his shoulder. His hands explored her body, the fullness of her breasts, the contour of her hips, the insides of her thighs. As his fingertips traced over her hips, she closed her eyes. Soon she was lost in touch, in the way his fingertips brushed across her skin, lost in this space with him where no harm could come to them and no obstacle could prevent them from being together.

Ethan's fingers dipped into her, gently exploring her depths and sending notes of arousal through her body. As Ethan entered her, pressing himself into her body, she gasped. His need swelled with an urgency, his breaths coming heavier. He slowed, stopped, pulled back before trying to press in again, more fully, until his hips pressed flush with her own. For Ophelia, the moment was a surrender, and she knew it was for Ethan as well.

When finally they lie still, Ethan whispered in her ear. "Are you all right?"

"I am," she said.

He grinned widely. "Oh, Ophelia. I could die that I didn't think of this sooner."

The realization swept over her as well. Here, they were safe to be together. When moving through time and space— when they were here in the *inbetween*—time did not exist. She could spend days with him and still return to the Maltorim's asylum within hours.

For all of Ethan's ability, she could return to Maltorim minutes before she'd even left, if she so chose.

"I will not live without ye," she said, pulling him closer.

"I will never ask it again," he promised.

To no longer have to deny her feelings sent a rush through Ophelia, and in that moment, Ophelia's heart fluttered in her chest. The heat between them intensified, and even the serpent's mark on her neck burned once again with ferocity. But she didn't care. Not now.

In these moments, she was human again.

Human, and very much in love.

If it were up to Ophelia, she would remain in his space, suspended for eternity with Ethan, her love, her sweetest downfall.

∼

Continue the Forever Girl Series in book one, The Forever Girl.

A YOUNG DESCENDENT of a true witch, Sophia discovers her familial curse can only be cured by entering a world of shifters, fae, and vampires who want her dead.

∾

Join Rebecca's newsletter for special deals, freebies, and giveaways!
https://rebeccahamilton.com/newsletter/

ABOUT THE AUTHOR

New York Times bestselling author Rebecca Hamilton writes urban fantasy and paranormal romance for Harlequin, Baste Lübbe, and Evershade. A book addict, registered bone marrow donor, and indian food enthusiast, she often takes to fictional worlds to see what perilous situations her characters will find themselves in next. Represented by Rossano Trentin of TZLA, Rebecca has been published internationally, in three languages: English, German, and Hungarian.

Read More from Rebecca
www.rebeccahamilton.com

www.ingramcontent.com/pod-product-compliance
Lightning Source LLC
Chambersburg PA
CBHW051922220626
47052CB00003B/552